RUDYARD KIPLING

Volume XIV

THE DAY'S WORK
卐 　 卐 　 Part II

"'Tain't much, though, is it?"

THE WRITINGS IN PROSE AND VERSE OF

RUDYARD KIPLING

THE DAY'S WORK

PART II

NEW YORK
CHARLES SCRIBNER'S SONS
1899

In rearranging my stories for the Outward Bound Edition I was careful to divide them into groups. This necessitated holding over several of the tales which were in design an integral part of "The Day's Work," till that book appeared. They will now be found in their proper places in these volumes.

RUDYARD KIPLING.

July 14, 1899.

CONTENTS

PART II

ILLUSTRATIONS

THE DAY'S WORK

PART II

.007

A LOCOMOTIVE is, next to a marine engine, the most sensitive thing man ever made; and No. .007, besides being sensitive, was new. The red paint was hardly dry on his spotless bumper-bar, his headlight shone like a fireman's helmet, and his cab might have been a hard-wood-finish parlour. They had run him into the round-house after his trial — he had said good-bye to his best friend in the shops, the overhead travelling-crane — the big world was just outside; and the other locos were taking stock of him. He looked at the semi-circle of bold, unwinking headlights, heard the low purr and mutter of the steam mounting in the gauges — scornful hisses of contempt as a slack valve lifted a little — and would have given a month's oil for leave to crawl through his own driving-wheels into the brick ash-pit beneath him. .007 was an eight-wheeled "American" loco, slightly different from others of his type, and as he stood he was worth ten thousand dollars on the Company's books. But if you had bought him at his own valuation, after half an hour's waiting in the darkish, echoing round-house, you would have saved exactly nine thousand nine hundred and ninety-nine dollars and ninety-eight cents.

A heavy Mogul freight, with a short cow-catcher and a fire-box that came down within three inches of the rail, began the impolite game, speaking to a Pittsburgh Consolidation, who was visiting.

"Where did this thing blow in from?" he asked, with a dreamy puff of light steam.

"It's all I can do to keep track of our makes," was the answer, "without lookin' after *your* back-numbers. 'Guess it's something Peter Cooper left over when he died."

.007 quivered; his steam was getting up, but he held his tongue. Even a hand-car knows what sort of locomotive it was that Peter Cooper experimented upon in the far-away Thirties. It carried its coal and water in two apple-barrels, and was not much bigger than a bicycle.

Then up and spoke a small, newish switching-engine, with a little step in front of his bumper-timber, and his wheels so close together that he looked like a bronco getting ready to buck.

"Something's wrong with the road when a Pennsylvania gravel-pusher tells us anything about our stock, *I* think. That kid's all right. Eustis designed him, and Eustis designed me. Ain't that good enough?"

.007 could have carried the switching-loco round

the yard in his tender, but he felt grateful for even this little word of consolation.

"We don't use hand-cars on the Pennsylvania," said the Consolidation. "That — er — peanut-stand's old enough and ugly enough to speak for himself."

"He hasn't bin spoken to yet. He's bin spoke *at*. Hain't ye any manners on the Pennsylvania?" said the switching-loco.

"You ought to be in the yard, Poney," said the Mogul, severely. "We're all long-haulers here."

"That's what you think," the little fellow replied. "You'll know more 'fore the night's out. I've bin down to Track 17, and the freight there — oh, Christmas!"

"I've trouble enough in my own division," said a lean, light suburban loco with very shiny brake-shoes. "My commuters wouldn't rest till they got a parlour-car. They've hitched it back of all, and it hauls worse'n a snow-plough. I'll snap her off some day sure, and then they'll blame every one except their fool-selves. They'll be askin' me to haul a vestibuled next!"

"They måde you in New Jersey, didn't they?" said Poney. "Thought so. Commuters and truck-wagons ain't any sweet haulin', but I tell *you* they're a heap better'n cuttin' out refrigerator-cars or oil-tanks. Why, I've hauled —"

"Haul! You?" said the Mogul, contemptu-
ously. "It's all you can do to bunt a cold-storage
car up the yard. Now, I—" he paused a little to
let the words sink in—"I handle the Flying
Freight—e-leven cars worth just anything you
please to mention. On the stroke of eleven I
pull out; and I'm timed for thirty-five an hour.
Costly—perishable—fragile—immediate—that's
me! Suburban traffic's only but one degree better than switching. Express freight's what pays."

"Well, I ain't given to blowing, as a rule,"
began the Pittsburgh Consolidation.

"No? You was sent in here because you
grunted on the grade," Poney interrupted.

"Where I grunt, you'd lie down, Poney: but,
as I was saying, I don't blow much. Notwith-
standin', *if* you want to see freight that is freight
moved lively, you should see me warbling through
the Alleghanies with thirty-seven ore-cars behind
me, and my brakemen fightin' tramps so 's they
can't attend to my tooter. I have to do all
the holdin' back then, and, though I say it, I've
never had a load get away from me yet. *No*,
sir. Haulin' 's one thing, but judgment and discretion 's another. You want judgment in my
business."

"Ah! But—but are you not paralysed by a
sense of your overwhelming responsibilities?"
said a curious, husky voice from a corner.

6

"Who's that?" .007 whispered to the Jersey commuter.

"Compound — experiment — N. G. She's bin switchin' in the B. & A. yards for six months, when she wasn't in the shops. She's economical (*I* call it mean) in her coal, but she takes it out in repairs. Ahem! I presume you found Boston somewhat isolated, madam, after your New York season?"

"I am never so well occupied as when I am alone." The Compound seemed to be talking from half-way up her smoke-stack.

"Sure," said the irreverent Poney, under his breath. "They don't hanker after her any in the yard."

"But, with my constitution and temperament — my work lies in Boston — I find your *outrecuidance —*"

"Outer which?" said the Mogul freight. "Simple cylinders are good enough for me."

"Perhaps I should have said *faroucherie,*" hissed the Compound.

"I don't hold with any make of papier-mâché wheel," the Mogul insisted.

The Compound sighed pityingly, and said no more.

"Git 'em all shapes in this world, don't ye?" said Poney. "That's Mass'chusetts all over. They half start, an' then they stick on a dead-centre, an' blame it all on other folks' ways o' treatin' them. Talkin' o' Boston, Comanche told me, last night, he had a hot-box just beyond the Newtons, Friday. That was why, *he* says, the Accommodation was held up. Made out no end of a tale, Comanche did."

"If I'd heard that in the shops, with my boiler out for repairs, I'd know 'twas one o' Comanche's lies," the New Jersey commuter snapped. "Hot-box! Him! What happened was they'd put an extra car on, and he just lay down on the grade and squealed. They had to send 127 to help him through. Made it out a hot-box, did he? Time before that he said he was ditched! Looked me square in the headlight and told me that as cool as — as a water-tank in a cold wave. Hot-box! You ask 127 about Comanche's hot-box. Why, Comanche he was side-tracked, and 127 (*he* was just about as mad as they make 'em on account o' being called out at ten o'clock at night) took hold and snapped her into Boston in seventeen minutes. Hot-box! Hot fraud! That's what Comanche is."

Then .007 put both drivers and his pilot into it, as the saying is, for he asked what sort of thing a hot-box might be?

"Paint my bell sky-blue!" said Poney, the switcher. "Make me a surface-railroad loco with a hard-wood skirtin'-board round my wheels.

Break me up and cast me into five-cent sidewalk-fakirs' mechanical toys! Here's an eight-wheel coupled 'American' don't know what a hot-box is! Never heard of an emergency-stop either, did ye? Don't know what ye carry jack-screws for? You're too innocent to be left alone with your own tender. Oh, you — you flat-car!"

There was a roar of escaping steam before any one could answer, and .007 nearly blistered his paint off with pure mortification.

"A hot-box," began the Compound, picking and choosing her words as though they were coal, "a hot-box is the penalty exacted from inexperience by haste. Ahem!"

"Hot-box!" said the Jersey Suburban. "It's the price you pay for going on the tear. It's years since I've had one. It's a disease that don't attack short-haulers, as a rule."

"We never have hot-boxes on the Pennsylvania," said the Consolidation. "They get 'em in New York — same as nervous prostration."

"Ah, go home on a ferry-boat," said the Mogul. "You think because you use worse grades than our road 'u'd allow, you're a kind of Alleghany angel. Now, I'll tell you what you . . . Here's my folk. Well, I can't stop. See you later, perhaps."

He rolled forward majestically to the turn-table, and swung like a man-of-war in a tideway, till he

9

picked up his track. "But as for you, you pea-green swivellin' coffee-pot (this to .007), you go out and learn something before you associate with those who've made more mileage in a week than you'll roll up in a year. Costly — perishable — fragile — immediate — that's me! S' long."

"Split my tubes if that's actin' polite to a new member o' the Brotherhood," said Poney. "There wasn't any call to trample on ye like that. But manners was left out when Moguls was made. Keep up your fire, kid, an' burn your own smoke. 'Guess we'll all be wanted in a minute."

Men were talking rather excitedly in the round-house. One man, in a dingy jersey, said that he hadn't any locomotives to waste on the yard. An-other man, with a piece of crumpled paper in his hand, said that the yard-master said that he was to say that if the other man said anything, he (the other man) was to shut his head. Then the other man waved his arms, and wanted to know if he was expected to keep locomotives in his hip-pocket. Then a man in a black Prince Albert, without a collar, came up dripping, for it was a hot August night, and said that what *he* said went; and between the three of them the locomotives began to go, too — first the Compound; then the Consolidation; then .007.

Now, deep down in his fire-box, .007 had cher-ished a hope that as soon as his trial was done, he would be led forth with songs and shoutings, and attached to a green-and-chocolate vestibuled flier, under charge of a bold and noble engineer, who would pat him on his back, and weep over him, and call him his Arab steed. (The boys in the shops where he was built used to read wonderful stories of railroad life, and .007 expected things to happen as he had heard.) But there did not seem to be many vestibuled fliers in the roaring, rumbling, electric-lighted yards, and his engineer only said:

"Now, what sort of a fool-sort of an injector has Eustis loaded on to this rig this time?" And he put the lever over with an angry snap, crying: "Am I supposed to switch with this thing, hey?"

The collarless man mopped his head, and replied that, in the present state of the yard and freight and a few other things, the engineer would switch and keep on switching till the cows came home. .007 pushed out gingerly, his heart in his headlight, so nervous that the clang of his own bell almost made him jump the track. Lanterns waved, or danced up and down, before and behind him; and on every side, six tracks deep, sliding backward and forward, with clashings of couplers and squeals of hand-brakes, were cars — more cars than .007 had dreamed of. There were oil-cars, and hay-cars, and stock-cars full of lowing beasts, and ore-cars, and potato-cars with stovepipe-ends sticking out in the middle; cold-storage and refrigerator cars dripping ice-water on the tracks; ventilated fruit- and milk-cars; flat-cars with truck-wagons full of market-stuff; flat-cars loaded with reapers and binders, all red and green and gilt under the sizzling electric lights; flat-cars piled high with strong-scented hides, pleasant hemlock-plank, or bundles of shingles; flat-cars creaking to the weight of thirty-ton castings, angle-irons, and rivet-boxes for some new bridge; and hundreds and hundreds and hundreds of box-cars loaded, locked, and chalked. Men — hot and angry — crawled among and between and under the thousand wheels; men took flying jumps through his cab, when he halted for a moment; men sat on his pilot as he went forward, and on his tender as he returned; and regiments of men ran along the tops of the box-cars beside him, screwing down brakes, waving their arms, and crying curious things.

He was pushed forward a foot at a time; whirled backward, his rear drivers clinking and clanking, a quarter of a mile; jerked into a switch (yard-switches are very stubby and unaccommodating), bunted into a Red D, or Merchant's Transport car, and, with no hint or knowledge of the weight behind him, started up anew. When his load was fairly on the move, three or four cars would be cut off, and .007 would bound forward, only to be held hiccupping on the brake. Then he would wait a few minutes, watching the whirled lanterns, deafened with the clang of the bells, giddy with the vision of the sliding cars, his brake-pump panting forty to the minute, his front coupler lying sideways on his cow-catcher, like a tired dog's tongue in his mouth, and the whole of him covered with half-burnt coal-dust.

" 'Tisn't so easy switching with a straight-backed tender," said his little friend of the round-house, bustling by at a trot. " But you're comin' on pretty fair. 'Ever seen a flyin' switch? No? Then watch me."

Poney was in charge of a dozen heady flat-cars. Suddenly he shot away from them with a sharp "*Whutt!*" A switch opened in the shadows ahead; he turned up it like a rabbit as it snapped behind him, and the long line of twelve-foot-high lumber jolted on into the arms of a full-sized road-loco, who acknowledged receipt with a dry howl.

" My man's reckoned the smartest in the yard at that trick," he said, returning. " 'Gives me cold shivers when another fool tries it, though. That's where my short wheel-base comes in. Like as not you'd have your tender scraped off if *you* tried it."

.007 had no ambitions that way, and said so.

" No? Of course this ain't your regular business, but say, don't you think it's interestin' ?

13

Have you seen the yard-master? Well, he's the greatest man on earth, an' don't you forget it. When are we through? Why, kid, it's always like this, day *an'* night — Sundays an' week-days. See that thirty-car freight slidin' in four, no, five tracks off? She's all mixed freight, sent here to be sorted out into straight trains. That's why we're cuttin' out the cars one by one." He gave a vigorous push to a west-bound car as he spoke, and started back with a little snort of surprise, for the car was an old friend — an M. T. K. box-car.

"Jack my drivers, but it's Homeless Kate! Why, Kate, ain't there *no* gettin' you back to your friends? There's forty chasers out for you from your road, if there's one. Who's holdin' you now?"

"Wish I knew," whimpered Homeless Kate. "I belong in Topeka, but I've bin to Cedar Rapids; I've bin to Winnipeg; I've bin to Newport News; I've bin all down the old Atlanta and West Point; an' I've bin to Buffalo. Maybe I'll fetch up at Haverstraw. I've only bin out ten months, but I'm homesick — I'm just achin' homesick."

"Try Chicago, Katie," said the switching-loco; and the battered old car lumbered down the track, jolting: "I want to be in Kansas when the sunflowers bloom."

14

" 'Yard's full o' Homeless Kates an' Wanderin'
Willies," he explained to .007. " I knew an old
Fitchburg flat-car out seventeen months; an' one
of ours was gone fifteen 'fore ever we got track of
her. Dunno quite how our men fix it. 'Swap
around, I guess. Anyway, I've done *my* duty.
She's on her way to Kansas, via Chicago; but I'll
lay my next boilerful she'll be held there to wait
consignee's convenience, and sent back to us with
wheat in the fall."

Just then the Pittsburgh Consolidation passed,
at the head of a dozen cars.

" I'm goin' home," he said proudly.

" 'Can't get all them twelve on to the flat.
Break 'em in half, Dutchy!" cried Poney. But it
was .007 who was backed down to the last six
cars, and he nearly blew up with surprise when he
found himself pushing them on to a huge ferry-
boat. He had never seen deep water before, and
shivered as the flat drew away and left his bogies
within six inches of the black, shiny tide.

After this he was hurried to the freight-house,
where he saw the yard-master, a smallish, white-
faced man in shirt, trousers, and slippers, looking
down upon a sea of trucks, a mob of bawling
truckmen, and squadrons of backing, turning,
sweating, spark-striking horses.

" That's shippers' carts loadin' on to the re-
ceivin' trucks," said the small engine, reverently.

15

"But *he* don't care. He lets 'em cuss. He's the Czar — King — Boss! He says 'Please,' and then they kneel down an' pray. There's three or four strings o' to-day's freight to be pulled before he can attend to *them*. When he waves his hand that way, things happen."

A string of loaded cars slid out down the track, and a string of empties took their place. Bales, crates, boxes, jars, carboys, frails, cases, and packages flew into them from the freight-house as though the cars had been magnets and they iron filings.

"Ki-yah!" shrieked little Poney. "Ain't it great?"

A purple-faced truckman shouldered his way to the yard-master, and shook his fist under his nose. The yard-master never looked up from his bundle of freight-receipts. He crooked his forefinger slightly, and a tall young man in a red shirt, lounging carelessly beside him, hit the truckman under the left ear, so that he dropped, quivering and clucking, on a hay-bale.

"Eleven, seven, ninety-seven, L. Y. S.; fourteen ought ought three; nineteen thirteen; one one four; seventeen ought twenty-one M. B.; *and* the ten west-bound. All straight except the two last. Cut 'em off at the junction. An' *that's* all right. Pull that string." The yard-master, with mild blue eyes, looked out over the howling truckmen at the waters in the moonlight beyond, and hummed:

> " All things bright and beautiful,
> All creatures great and small,
> *All* things wise and wonderful,
> The Lawd Gawd He made all ! "

.007 moved out the cars and delivered them to the regular road-engine. He had never felt quite so limp in his life before.

"Curious, ain't it?" said Poney, puffing, on the next track. "You an' me, if we got that man under our bumpers, we'd work him into red waste an' not know what we'd done; but — up there — with the steam hummin' in his boiler that awful quiet way . . ."

"*I* know," said .007. "Makes me feel as if I'd dropped my fire an' was getting cold. He is the greatest man on earth."

They were at the far north end of the yard now, under a switch-tower, looking down on the four-track way of the main traffic. The Boston Compound was to haul .007's string to some far-away northern junction over an indifferent road-bed, and she mourned aloud for the ninety-six-pound rails of the B. & A.

"You're young; you're young," she coughed. "You don't realise your responsibilities."

"Yes, he does," said Poney, sharply; "but he don't lie down under 'em." Then, with a side-

spurt of steam, exactly like a tough spitting:
"There ain't more than fifteen thousand dollars' worth o' freight behind her anyway, and
she goes on as if 'twere a hundred thousand —
same as the Mogul's. Excuse me, madam,
but you've the track. . . . She's stuck on a
dead-centre again — bein' specially designed
not to."

The Compound crawled across the tracks on a
long slant, groaning horribly at each switch, and
moving like a cow in a snow-drift. There was a
little pause along the yard after her tail-lights had
disappeared; switches locked crisply, and every
one seemed to be waiting.

"Now I'll show you something worth," said
Poney. "When the Purple Emperor ain't on
time, it's about time to amend the Constitution.
The first stroke of twelve is —"

"Boom!" went the clock in the big yard-tower,
and far away .007 heard a full, vibrating *"Yah!
Yah! Yah!"* A headlight twinkled on the horizon like a star, grew an overpowering blaze, and
whooped up the humming track to the roaring
music of a happy giant's song:

"With a michnai — ghignai — shtingal! Yah! Yah! Yah!
  Ein — zwei — drei — Mutter! Yah! Yah! Yah!
      She climb upon der shteeple,
      Und she frighten all der people.
  Singin' michnai — ghignai — shtingal ! Yah! Yah!"

The last defiant "yah! yah!" was delivered a mile and a half beyond the passenger-depot; but .007 had caught one glimpse of the superb six-wheeled-coupled racing-locomotive, who hauled the pride and glory of the road—the gilt-edged Purple Emperor, the millionaires' south-bound express, laying the miles over his shoulder as a man peels a shaving from a soft board. The rest was a blur of maroon enamel, a bar of white light from the electrics in the cars, and a flicker of nickel-plated hand-rail on the rear platform.

"Ooh!" said .007.

"Seventy-five miles an hour these five miles. Baths, I've heard; barber's shop; ticker; and a library and the rest to match. Yes, sir; seventy-five an hour! But he'll talk to you in the round-house just as democratic as I would. And I — cuss my wheel-base! — I'd kick clean off the track at half his gait. He's the Master of our Lodge. Cleans up at our house. I'll introdooce you some day. He's worth knowin'! There ain't many can sing that song, either."

.007 was too full of emotions to answer. He did not hear a raging of telephone-bells in the switch-tower, nor the man, as he leaned out and called to .007's engineer: "'Got any steam?"

"'Nough to run her a hundred mile out o' this, if I could," said the engineer, who belonged to the open road and hated switching.

" Then get. The Flying Freight's ditched forty mile out, with fifty rod o' track ploughed up. No; no one's hurt, but both tracks are blocked. Lucky the wreckin'-car an' derrick are this end of the yard. Crew'll be along in a minute. Hurry! You've the track."

" Well, I could jest kick my little sawed-off self," said Poney, as .007 was backed, with a bang, on to a grim and grimy car like a caboose, but full of tools — a flat-car and a derrick behind it. "Some folks are one thing, and some are another; but *you're* in luck, kid. They push a wrecking-car. Now, don't get rattled. Your wheel-base will keep you on the track, and there ain't any curves worth mentionin'. Oh, say! Comanche told me there's one section o' saw-edged track that's liable to jounce ye a little. Fifteen an' a half out, *after* the grade at Jackson's crossin'. You'll know it by a farm-house an' a windmill an' five maples in the dooryard. 'Windmill's west o' the maples. An' there's an eighty-foot iron bridge in the middle o' that section with no guard-rails. See you later. Luck!"

Before he knew well what had happened, .007 was flying up the track into the dumb, dark world. Then fears of the night beset him. He remembered all he had ever heard of landslides, rain-piled boulders, blown trees, and strayed cattle, all that the Boston Compound had ever said of responsi-

20

bility, and a great deal more that came out of his own head. With a very quavering voice he whistled for his first grade-crossing (an event in the life of a locomotive), and his nerves were in no way restored by the sight of a frantic horse and a white-faced man in a buggy less than a yard from his right shoulder. Then he was sure he would jump the track; felt his flanges mounting the rail at every curve; knew that his first grade would make him lie down even as Comanche had done at the Newtons. He whirled down the grade to Jackson's crossing, saw the windmill west of the maples, felt the badly laid rails spring under him, and sweated big drops all over his boiler. At each jarring bump he believed an axle had smashed, and he took the eighty-foot bridge without the guard-rail like a hunted cat on the top of a fence. Then a wet leaf stuck against the glass of his headlight and threw a flying shadow on the track, so that he thought it was some little dancing animal that would feel soft if he ran over it; and anything soft underfoot frightens a locomotive as it does an elephant. But the men behind seemed quite calm. The wrecking-crew were climbing carelessly from the caboose to the tender — even jesting with the engineer, for he heard a shuffling of feet among the coal, and the snatch of a song, something like this:

"Oh, the Empire State must learn to wait,
And the Cannon-ball go hang!
When the West-bound's ditched, and the tool-car's hitched,
And it's 'way for the Breakdown Gang (Tara-ra!)
'Way for the Breakdown Gang!"

"Say! Eustis knew what he was doin' when he designed this rig. She's a hummer. New, too."

"Snff! Phew! She *is* new. That ain't paint. That's —"

A burning pain shot through .007's right rear driver — a crippling, stinging pain.

"This," said .007, as he flew, "is a hot-box. Now I know what it means. I shall go to pieces, I guess. My first road-run, too!"

"Het a bit, ain't she?" the fireman ventured to suggest to the engineer.

"She'll hold for all we want of her. We're 'most there. 'Guess you chaps back had better climb into your car," said the engineer, his hand on the brake-lever. "I've seen men snapped off —"

But the crew fled back with laughter. They had no wish to be jerked on to the track. The engineer half turned his wrist, and .007 found his drivers pinned firm.

"Now it's come!" said .007, as he yelled aloud, and slid like a sleigh. For the moment he fancied that he would jerk bodily from off his underpinning.

"That must be the emergency-stop that Poney guyed me about," he gasped, as soon as he could think. " Hot-box — emergency-stop. They both hurt; but now I can talk back in the round-house."

He was halted, all hissing hot, a few feet in the rear of what doctors would call a compound-comminuted car. His engineer was kneeling down among his drivers, but he did not call .007 his " Arab steed," nor cry over him, as the engineers did in the newspapers. He just bad-worded .007, and pulled yards of charred cotton-waste from about the axles, and hoped he might some day catch the idiot who had packed it. Nobody else attended to him, for Evans, the Mogul's engineer, a little cut about the head, but very angry, was exhibiting, by lantern-light, the mangled corpse of a slim blue pig.

" 'Tweren't even a decent-sized hog," he said. " 'Twere a shote."

" Dangerousest beasts they are," said one of the crew. " Get under the pilot an' sort o' twiddle ye off the track, don't they ? "

" Don't they ? " roared Evans, who was a red-headed Welshman. " You talk as if I was ditched by a hog every fool-day o' the week. *I* ain't friends with all the cussed half-fed shotes in the State o' New York. No, indeed ! Yes, this is him — an' look what he's done ! "

It was not a bad night's work for one stray piglet. The Flying Freight seemed to have flown in every direction, for the Mogul had mounted the rails and run diagonally a few hundred feet from right to left, taking with him such cars as cared to follow. Some did not. They broke their couplers and lay down, while rear cars frolicked over them. In that game, they had ploughed up and removed and twisted a good deal of the left-hand track. The Mogul himself had waddled into a corn-field, and there he knelt — fantastic wreaths of green twisted round his crank-pins; his pilot covered with solid clods of field, on which corn nodded drunkenly; his fire put out with dirt (Evans had done that as soon as he recovered his senses); and his broken headlight half full of half-burnt moths. His tender had thrown coal all over him, and he looked like a disreputable buffalo who had tried to wallow in a general store. For there lay scattered over the landscape, from the burst cars, type-writers, sewing-machines, bicycles in crates, a consignment of silver-plated imported harness, French dresses and gloves, a dozen finely moulded hard-wood mantels, a fifteen-foot naphtha-launch, with a solid brass bedstead crumpled around her bows, a case of telescopes and microscopes, two coffins, a case of very best candies, some gilt-edged dairy produce, butter and eggs in an omelette, a broken box of expensive toys, and a few hundred other luxuries. A camp of tramps hurried up from nowhere, and generously volunteered to help the crew. So the brakemen, armed with coupler-pins, walked up and down on one side, and the freight-conductor and the fireman patrolled the other with their hands in their hip-pockets. A long-bearded man came out of a house beyond the corn-field, and told Evans that if the accident had happened a little later in the year, all his corn would have been burned, and accused Evans of carelessness. Then he ran away, for Evans was at his heels shrieking: "'Twas his hog done it — his hog done it! Let me kill him! Let me kill him!" Then the wrecking-crew laughed; and the farmer put his head out of a window and said that Evans was no gentleman.

But .007 was very sober. He had never seen a wreck before, and it frightened him. The crew still laughed, but they worked at the same time; and .007 forgot horror in amazement at the way they handled the Mogul freight. They dug round him with spades; they put ties in front of his wheels, and jack-screws under him; they embraced him with the derrick-chain and tickled him with crow-bars; while .007 was hitched on to wrecked cars and backed away till the knot broke or the cars rolled clear of the track. By dawn thirty or forty men were at work, replacing and ramming down the ties, gauging the rails and spiking them. By daylight all cars who could move had gone on in charge of another loco; the track was freed for traffic; and .007 had hauled the old Mogul over a small pavement of ties, inch by inch, till his flanges bit the rail once more, and he settled down with a clank. But his spirit was broken, and his nerve was gone.

" 'Tweren't even a hog," he repeated dolefully; " 'twere a shote; and you — *you* of all of 'em — had to help me on."

"But how in the whole long road did it happen?" asked .007, sizzling with curiosity.

"Happen! It didn't happen! It just come! I sailed right on top of him around that last curve — thought he was a skunk. Yes; he was all as little as that. He hadn't more'n squealed once 'fore I felt my bogies lift (he'd rolled right under the pilot), and I couldn't catch the track again to save me. Swivelled clean off, I was. Then I felt him sling himself along, all greasy, under my left leadin' driver, and, oh, Boilers! that mounted the rail. I heard my flanges zippin' along the ties, an' the next I knew I was playin' 'Sally, Sally Waters' in the corn, my tender shuckin' coal through my cab, an' old man Evans lyin' still an' bleedin' in front o' me. Shook? There ain't a stay or a bolt or a rivet in me that ain't sprung to glory somewhere."

"Umm!" said .007. "What d' you reckon you weigh?"

"Without these lumps o' dirt I'm all of a hundred thousand pound."

"And the shote?"

26

"Eighty. Call him a hundred pound at the outside. He's worth about four 'n' a half dollars. Ain't it awful? Ain't it enough to give you nervous prostration? Ain't it paralysin'? Why, I come just around that curve — " and the Mogul told the tale again, for he was very badly shaken.

"Well, it's all in the day's run, I guess," said .007, soothingly; "an'— an' a corn-field's pretty soft fallin'."

"If it had bin a sixty-foot bridge, an' I could ha' slid off into deep water an' blown up an' killed both men, same as others have done, I wouldn't ha' cared; but to be ditched by a shote — an' you to help me out — in a corn-field — an' an old hay-seed in his nightgown cussin' me like as if I was a sick truck-horse! . . . Oh, it's awful! Don't call me Mogul! I'm a sewin'-machine. They'll guy my sand-box off in the yard."

And .007, his hot-box cooled and his experience vastly enlarged, hauled the Mogul freight slowly to the round-house.

"Hello, old man! Bin out all night, hain't ye?" said the irrepressible Poney, who had just come off duty. "Well, I must say you look it. Costly — perishable — fragile — immediate — that's you! Go to the shops, take them vine-leaves out o' your hair, an' git 'em to play the hose on you."

"Leave him alone, Poney," said .007, severely, as he was swung on the turn-table, " or I'll — "

27

"'Didn't know the old granger was any special friend o' yours, kid. He wasn't over-civil to you last time I saw him."

"I know it; but I've seen a wreck since then, and it has about scared the paint off me. I'm not going to guy any one as long as I steam — not when they're new to the business an' anxious to learn. And I'm not goin' to guy the old Mogul either, though I did find him wreathed around with roastin'-ears. 'Twas a little bit of a shote — not a hog — just a shote, Poney — no bigger'n a lump of anthracite — I saw it — that made all the mess. Anybody can be ditched, I guess."

"'Found that out already, have you? Well, that's a good beginnin'." It was the Purple Emperor, with his high, tight, plate-glass cab and green-velvet cushion, waiting to be cleaned for his next day's fly.

"Let me make you two gen'lemen acquainted," said Poney. "This is our Purple Emperor, kid, whom you were admirin' and, I may say, envyin' last night. This is a new brother, worshipful sir, with most of his mileage ahead of him, but, so far as a serving-brother can, I'll answer for him."

"'Happy to meet you," said the Purple Emperor, with a glance round the crowded roundhouse. "I guess there are enough of us here to form a full meetin'. Ahem! By virtue of the authority vested in me as Head of the Road, I hereby declare and pronounce No. .007 a full and accepted Brother of the Amalgamated Brotherhood of Locomotives, and as such entitled to all shop, switch, track, tank, and round-house privileges throughout my jurisdiction, in the Degree of Superior Flier, it bein' well known and credibly reported to me that our Brother has covered forty-one miles in thirty-nine minutes and a half on an errand of mercy to the afflicted. At a convenient time, I myself will communicate to you the Song and Signal of this Degree whereby you may be recognised in the darkest night. Take your stall, newly entered Brother among Locomotives!"

* * * * * * * * * *

Now, in the darkest night, even as the Purple Emperor said, if you will stand on the bridge across the freight-yard, looking down upon the four-track way, at 2:30 A. M., neither before nor after, when the White Moth, that takes the overflow from the Purple Emperor, tears south with her seven vestibuled cream-white cars, you will hear, as the yard-clock makes the half-hour, a faraway sound like the bass of a violoncello, and then, a hundred feet to each word:

"With a michnai — ghignai — shtingal! Yah! Yah! Yah!
Ein — zwei — drei — Mutter! Yah! Yah! Yah!

29

She climb upon der shteeple,
Und she frighten all der people,
Singin' michnai — ghignai — shtingal! Yah! Yah!"

That is .007 covering his one hundred and fifty-six miles in two hundred and twenty-one minutes.

THE WRECK OF THE "VISIGOTH"

THE WRECK OF THE "VISIGOTH"[1]

"Eternal Father, strong to save,
Whose arm hath bound the restless wave,
Who bidst the mighty ocean keep
Its own appointed limits deep."

THE lady passengers were trying the wheezy old harmonium in front of the cuddy, because it was Sunday night. In the patch of darkness near the wheel-grating sat the Captain, and the end of his cheroot burned like a head-lamp. There was neither breath nor motion upon the waters through which the screw was thudding. They spread, dull silver, under the haze of the moonlight till they joined the low coast of Malacca away to the eastward. The voices of the singers at the harmonium were held down by the awnings, and came to us with force.

"Oh, hear us when we cry to Thee,
For those in peril on the sea!"

It was as though the little congregation were afraid of the vastness of the sea. But a laugh followed, and some one said, "Shall we take it

1 Copyright, 1895, by Macmillan & Co.

through again a little quicker?" Then the Captain told the story of just such a night, lowering his voice for fear of disturbing the music and the minds of the passengers.

"She was the *Visigoth*,— five hundred tons, or it may have been six,— in the coasting trade; one of the best steamers and best found on the Kutch-Kasauli line. She wasn't six years old when the thing happened : on just such a night as this, with an oily-smooth sea, under brilliant starlight, about a hundred miles from land. To this day no one knows really what the matter was. She was so small that she could not have struck even a log in the water without every soul on board feeling the jar; and even if she had struck something, it wouldn't have made her go down as she did. I was fourth officer then; we had about seven saloon passengers, including the Captain's wife and another woman, and perhaps five hundred deck-passengers going up the coast to a shrine, on just such a night as this, when she was ripping through the level sea at a level nine knots an hour. The man on the bridge, whoever it was, saw that she was sinking at the head. Sinking by the head as she went along. That was the only warning we got. She began to sink as she went along. Of course the Captain was told, and he sent me to wake up the saloon passengers and tell them to come on deck. 'Sounds a curious sort of message that to deliver on a dead-still night. The people tumbled up in their dressing-gowns and *pyjamas*, and wouldn't believe me. We were just sinking as fast as we could, and I had to tell 'em that. Then the deck-passengers got wind of it, and all Hell woke up along the decks.

" The rule in these little affairs is to get your saloon passengers off first, then to fill the boats with the balance, and afterwards—God help the extras, that's all. I was getting the starboard stern boat — the mail-boat — away. It hung as it might be over yonder, and as I came along from the cuddy, the deck-passengers hung round me, shoving their money-belts into my hand, taking off their nose-rings and ear-rings, and thrusting 'em upon me to buy just one chance for life. If I hadn't been so desperately busy, I should have thought it horrible. I put biscuits and water into the boat, and got the two ladies in. One of 'em was the Captain's wife. She had to be put in by main force. You've no notion how women can struggle. The other woman was the wife of an officer going to meet her husband; and there were a couple of passengers beside the lascars. The Captain said he was going to stay with the ship. You see the rule in these affairs, I believe, is that the Captain has to bow gracefully from the bridge and go down. I haven't had a ship under my charge wrecked yet. When that comes, I'll have to do like the others. After the boats were away, and I saw that there was nothing to be got by waiting, I jumped overboard exactly as I might have vaulted over into a flat green field, and struck out for the mail-boat. Another officer did the same thing, but he went for a boat full of natives, and they whacked him on the chest with oars, so he had some difficulty in climbing in.

"It was as well that I reached the mail-boat. There was a compass in it, but the idiots had managed to fill the boat half full of water somehow or another, and none of the crew seemed to know what was required of them. Then the *Visigoth* went down and took every one with her — ships generally do that; the corpses don't cumber the sea for some time.

"What did I do? I kept all the boats together, and headed into the track of the coasting steamers. The aggravating thing was the thought that we were close to land as far as a big steamer was concerned, and in the middle of eternity as far as regarded a little boat. The sea looks hugeous big from a boat at night."

> "Oh, Christ, whose voice the waters heard
> And hushed their ravings at Thy word,
> Who walkedst on the foaming deep
> And calm amidst its rage did keep,—
> Oh, hear us when we cry to Thee,
> For those in peril on the sea!"

sang the passengers cheerily.

"That harmonium is disgracefully out of tune,"

said the Captain. " The sea air affects their insides.
Well, as I was saying, we settled down in the boat.
The Captain's wife was unconscious; she lay in
the bottom of the boat and moaned. I was glad
she wasn't threshing about the boat: but what I
did think was wrong, was the way the two men
passengers behaved. They were useless with
funk — out-and-out fear. They lay in the boat
and did nothing. Fetched a groan now and again
to show they were alive; but that was all. But
the other woman was a jewel. Damn it, it was
worth being shipwrecked to have that woman in
the boat; she was awfully handsome, and as brave
as she was lovely. She helped me bail out the
boat, and she worked like a man.

" So we kicked about the sea from midnight till
seven the next evening, and then we saw a steamer.
'I'll — I'll give you anything I'm wearing to hoist
as a signal of distress,' said the woman; but I had
no need to ask her, for the steamer picked us up
and took us back to Bombay. I forgot to tell you
that, when the day broke, I couldn't recognise the
Captain's wife — widow, I mean. She had changed
in the night as if fire had gone over her. I met
her a long time afterwards, and even then she
hadn't forgiven me for putting her into the boat and
obeying the Captain's orders. But the husband
of the other woman — he's in the Army — wrote
me no end of a letter of thanks. I don't suppose
he considered that the way his wife behaved was

enough to make any decent man do all he could. The other fellows, who lay in the bottom of the boat and groaned, I've never met. 'Don't want to. 'Shouldn't be civil to 'em if I did. And that's how the *Visigoth* went down, for no assignable reason, with eighty bags of mail, five hundred souls, and not a single packet insured, on just such a night as this."

> " Oh, Trinity of love and power,
>   Our brethren shield in that dread hour,
>   From rock and tempest, fire and foe,
>   Protect them wheresoe'er they go.
>   Thus evermore shall rise to Thee
>   Glad hymns of praise by land and sea."

"'Strikes me they'll go on singing that hymn all night. 'Imperfect sort of doctrine in the last lines, don't you think? They might have run in an extra verse specifying sudden collapse—like the *Visigoth's*. I'm going on to the bridge, now. Good night," said the Captain.

And I was left alone with the steady thud, thud, of the screw and the gentle creaking of the boats at the davits.

That made me shudder.

THE MALTESE CAT

THE MALTESE CAT

THEY had good reason to be proud, and better reason to be afraid, all twelve of them; for though they had fought their way, game by game, up the teams entered for the polo tournament, they were meeting the Archangels that afternoon in the final match; and the Archangels men were playing with half a dozen ponies apiece. As the game was divided into six quarters of eight minutes each, that meant a fresh pony after every halt. The Skidars' team, even supposing there were no accidents, could only supply one pony for every other change; and two to one is heavy odds. Again, as Shiraz, the grey Syrian, pointed out, they were meeting the pink and pick of the polo-ponies of Upper India, ponies that had cost from a thousand rupees each, while they themselves were a cheap lot gathered, often from country-carts, by their masters, who belonged to a poor but honest native infantry regiment.

"Money means pace and weight," said Shiraz, rubbing his black-silk nose dolefully along his

41

neat-fitting boot, "and by the maxims of the game as I know it — "

"Ah, but we aren't playing the maxims," said The Maltese Cat. "We're playing the game; and we've the great advantage of knowing the game. Just think a stride, Shiraz! We've pulled up from bottom to second place in two weeks against all those fellows on the ground here. That's because we play with our heads as well as our feet."

"It makes me feel undersized and unhappy all the same," said Kittiwynk, a mouse-coloured mare with a red brow-band and the cleanest pair of legs that ever an aged pony owned. "They've twice our style, these others."

Kittiwynk looked at the gathering and sighed. The hard, dusty polo-ground was lined with thousands of soldiers, black and white, not counting hundreds and hundreds of carriages and drags and dog-carts, and ladies with brilliant-coloured parasols, and officers in uniform and out of it, and crowds of natives behind them; and orderlies on camels, who had halted to watch the game, instead of carrying letters up and down the station; and native horse-dealers running about on thin-eared Biluchi mares, looking for a chance to sell a few first-class polo-ponies. Then there were the ponies of thirty teams that had entered for the Upper India Free-for-All Cup — nearly every pony of worth and dignity, from Mhow to Peshawur, from Allahabad to Multan; prize ponies, Arabs, Syrian, Barb, country-bred, Deccanee, Waziri, and Kabul ponies of every colour and shape and temper that you could imagine. Some of them were in mat-roofed stables, close to the polo-ground, but most were under saddle, while their masters, who had been defeated in the earlier games, trotted in and out and told the world exactly how the game should be played.

It was a glorious sight, and the come and go of the little, quick hooves, and the incessant salutations of ponies that had met before on other polo-grounds or race-courses, were enough to drive a four-footed thing wild.

But the Skidars' team were careful not to know their neighbours, though half the ponies on the ground were anxious to scrape acquaintance with the little fellows that had come from the North, and, so far, had swept the board.

" Let's see," said a soft gold-coloured Arab, who had been playing very badly the day before, to The Maltese Cat; "didn't we meet in Abdul Rahman's stable in Bombay, four seasons ago? I won the Paikpattan Cup next season, you may remember?"

"Not me," said The Maltese Cat, politely. "I was at Malta then, pulling a vegetable-cart. I don't race. I play the game."

"Oh!" said the Arab, cocking his tail and swaggering off.

"Keep yourselves to yourselves," said The Maltese Cat to his companions. "We don't want to rub noses with all those goose-rumped half-breeds of Upper India. When we've won this Cup they'll give their shoes to know *us*."

"We sha'n't win the Cup," said Shiraz. "How do you feel?"

"Stale as last night's feed when a muskrat has run over it," said Polaris, a rather heavy-shouldered grey; and the rest of the team agreed with him.

"The sooner you forget that the better," said The Maltese Cat, cheerfully. "They've finished tiffin in the big tent. We shall be wanted now. If your saddles are not comfy, kick. If your bits aren't easy, rear, and let the *saises* know whether your boots are tight."

Each pony had his *sais*, his groom, who lived and ate and slept with the animal, and had betted a good deal more than he could afford on the result of the game. There was no chance of anything going wrong, but to make sure, each *sais* was shampooing the legs of his pony to the last minute. Behind the *saises* sat as many of the Skidars' regiment as had leave to attend the match — about half the native officers, and a hundred or two dark, black-bearded men, with the regimental pipers nervously fingering the big, beribboned bagpipes. The Skidars were what they call a Pioneer regiment, and the bagpipes made the national music of half their men. The native officers held bundles of polo-sticks, long cane-handled mallets, and as the grand stand filled after lunch they arranged themselves by ones and twos at different points round the ground, so that if a stick were broken the player would not have far to ride for a new one. An impatient British Cavalry Band struck up "If you want to know the time, ask a p'leeceman!" and the two umpires in light dust-coats danced out on two little excited ponies. The four players of the Archangels' team followed, and the sight of their beautiful mounts made Shiraz groan again.

"Wait till we know," said The Maltese Cat. "Two of 'em are playing in blinkers, and that means they can't see to get out of the way of their own side, or they *may* shy at the umpires' ponies. They've *all* got white web-reins that are sure to stretch or slip!"

"And," said Kittiwynk, dancing to take the stiffness out of her, "they carry their whips in their hands instead of on their wrists. Hah!"

"True enough. No man can manage his stick and his reins and his whip that way," said The Maltese Cat. "I've fallen over every square yard of the Malta ground, and I ought to know."

He quivered his little, flea-bitten withers just to show how satisfied he felt; but his heart was not so light. Ever since he had drifted into India on a troop-ship, taken, with an old rifle, as part payment for a racing debt, The Maltese Cat had played and preached polo to the Skidars' team on the Skidars' stony polo-ground. Now a polo-pony is like a poet. If he is born with a love for the game, he can be made. The Maltese Cat knew that bamboos grew solely in order that polo-balls might be turned from their roots, that grain was given to ponies to keep them in hard condition, and that ponies were shod to prevent them slipping on a turn. But, besides all these things, he knew every trick and device of the finest game in the world, and for two seasons had been teaching the others all he knew or guessed.

"Remember," he said for the hundredth time, as the riders came up, "you *must* play together, and you *must* play with your heads. Whatever happens, follow the ball. Who goes out first?"

Kittiwynk, Shiraz, Polaris, and a short high little bay fellow with tremendous hocks and no withers worth speaking of (he was called Corks) were being girthed up, and the soldiers in the background stared with all their eyes.

"I want you men to keep quiet," said Lutyens, the captain of the team, "and especially not to blow your pipes."

"Not if we win, Captain Sahib?" asked the piper.

"If we win you can do what you please," said Lutyens, with a smile, as he slipped the loop of his stick over his wrist, and wheeled to canter to his place. The Archangels' ponies were a little bit above themselves on account of the many-coloured crowd so close to the ground. Their riders were excellent players, but they were a team of crack players instead of a crack team; and that made all the difference in the world. They honestly meant to play together, but it is very hard for four men, each the best of the team he is picked from, to remember that in polo no brilliancy in hitting or riding makes up for playing alone. Their captain shouted his orders to them by name, and it is a curious thing that if you call his name aloud in public after an Englishman you make him hot and fretty. Lutyens said nothing to his men, because it had all been said before. He pulled up Shiraz, for he was playing "back," to guard the goal. Powell on Polaris was half-back, and Macnamara and Hughes on Corks and Kittiwynk were forwards. The tough, bamboo ball was set in the middle of the ground, one hundred and fifty yards from the ends, and Hughes crossed sticks, heads up, with the Captain of the Archangels, who saw fit to play forward; that is a place from which you cannot easily control your team.

The little click as the cane-shafts met was heard all over the ground, and then Hughes made some sort of quick wrist-stroke that just dribbled the ball a few yards. Kittiwynk knew that stroke of old, and followed as a cat follows a mouse. While the Captain of the Archangels was wrenching his pony round, Hughes struck with all his strength, and next instant Kittiwynk was away, Corks following close behind her, their little feet pattering like raindrops on glass.

"Pull out to the left," said Kittiwynk between her teeth; "it's coming your way, Corks!"

The back and half-back of the Archangels were tearing down on her just as she was within reach of the ball. Hughes leaned forward with a loose rein, and cut it away to the left almost under Kittiwynk's foot, and it hopped and skipped off to Corks, who saw that if he was not quick it would run beyond the boundaries. That long bouncing drive gave the Archangels time to wheel and send three men across the ground to head off Corks. Kittiwynk stayed where she was; for she knew the game. Corks was on the ball half a fraction of a second before the others came up, and Macnamara, with a backhanded stroke, sent it back across the ground to Hughes, who saw the way clear to the Archangels' goal, and smacked the ball in before any one quite knew what had happened.

"That's luck," said Corks, as they changed ends. "A goal in three minutes for three hits, and no riding to speak of."

"'Don't know," said Polaris. "We've made 'em angry too soon. 'Shouldn't wonder if they tried to rush us off our feet next time."

"Keep the ball hanging, then," said Shiraz. "That wears out every pony that is not used to it."

Next time there was no easy galloping across the ground. All the Archangels closed up as one man, but there they stayed, for Corks, Kittiwynk, and Polaris were somewhere on the top of the ball, marking time among the rattling sticks, while Shiraz circled about outside, waiting for a chance.

"We can do this all day," said Polaris, ramming his quarters into the side of another pony. "Where do you think you're shoving to?"

"I'll — I'll be driven in an *ekka* if I know," was the gasping reply, "and I'd give a week's feed to get my blinkers off. I can't see anything."

"The dust is rather bad. Whew! That was one for my off-hock. Where's the ball, Corks?"

"Under my tail. At least, the man's looking for it there! This is beautiful. They can't use their sticks, and it's driving 'em wild. Give old Blinkers a push and then he'll go over."

"Here, don't touch me! I can't see. I'll — I'll back out, I think," said the pony in blinkers, who knew that if you can't see all round your head, you cannot prop yourself against the shock.

Corks was watching the ball where it lay in the dust, close to his near fore-leg, with Macnamara's shortened stick tap-tapping it from time to time. Kittiwynk was edging her way out of the scrimmage, whisking her stump of a tail with nervous excitement.

"Ho! They've got it," she snorted. "Let me out!" and she galloped like a rifle-bullet just behind a tall lanky pony of the Archangels, whose rider was swinging up his stick for a stroke.

"Not to-day, thank you," said Hughes, as the blow slid off his raised stick, and Kittiwynk laid her shoulder to the tall pony's quarters, and shoved him aside just as Lutyens on Shiraz sent the ball where it had come from, and the tall pony went skating and slipping away to the left. Kittiwynk, seeing that Polaris had joined Corks in the chase for the ball up the ground, dropped into Polaris' place, and then "time" was called.

The Skidars' ponies wasted no time in kicking or fuming. They knew that each minute's rest meant so much gain, and trotted off to the rails, and their *saises* began to scrape and blanket and rub them at once.

"Whew!" said Corks, stiffening up to get all the tickle of the big vulcanite scraper. "If we were playing pony for pony, we would bend those

Archangels double in half an hour. But they'll bring up fresh ones and fresh ones and fresh ones after that — you see."

"Who cares?" said Polaris. "We've drawn first blood. Is my hock swelling?"

"'Looks puffy," said Corks. "You must have had rather a wipe. Don't let it stiffen. You'll be wanted again in half an hour."

"What's the game like?" said The Maltese Cat.

"'Ground's like your shoe, except where they put too much water on it," said Kittiwynk. "Then it's slippery. Don't play in the centre. There's a bog there. I don't know how their next four are going to behave, but we kept the ball hanging, and made 'em lather for nothing. Who goes out? Two Arabs and a couple of country-breds! That's bad. What a comfort it is to wash your mouth out!"

Kitty was talking with a neck of a lather-covered soda-water bottle between her teeth, and trying to look over her withers at the same time. This gave her a very coquettish air.

"What's bad?" said Grey Dawn, giving to the girth and admiring his well-set shoulders.

"You Arabs can't gallop fast enough to keep yourselves warm — that's what Kitty means," said Polaris, limping to show that his hock needed attention. "Are you playing back, Grey Dawn?"

"'Looks like it," said Grey Dawn, as Lutyens swung himself up. Powell mounted The Rabbit, a plain bay country-bred much like Corks, but with mulish ears. Macnamara took Faiz-Ullah, a handy, short-backed little red Arab with a long tail, and Hughes mounted Benami, an old and sullen brown beast, who stood over in front more than a polo-pony should.

"Benami looks like business," said Shiraz. "How's your temper, Ben?" The old campaigner hobbled off without answering, and The Maltese Cat looked at the new Archangel ponies prancing about on the ground. They were four beautiful blacks, and they saddled big enough and strong enough to eat the Skidars' team and gallop away with the meal inside them.

"Blinkers again," said The Maltese Cat. "Good enough!"

"They're chargers — cavalry chargers!" said Kittiwynk, indignantly. "*They'll* never see thirteen three again."

"They've all been fairly measured, and they've all got their certificates," said The Maltese Cat, "or they wouldn't be here. We must take things as they come along, and keep your eyes on the ball."

The game began, but this time the Skidars were penned to their own end of the ground, and the watching ponies did not approve of that.

" Faiz-Ullah is shirking — as usual," said Polaris, with a scornful grunt.

" Faiz-Ullah is eating whip," said Corks. They could hear the leather-thonged polo-quirt lacing the little fellow's well-rounded barrel. Then The Rabbit's shrill neigh came across the ground.

" I can't do all the work," he cried desperately.

" Play the game — don't talk," The Maltese Cat whickered ; and all the ponies wriggled with excitement, and the soldiers and the grooms gripped the railings and shouted. A black pony with blinkers had singled out old Benami, and was interfering with him in every possible way. They could see Benami shaking his head up and down, and flapping his under lip.

" There'll be a fall in a minute," said Polaris. " Benami is getting stuffy."

The game flickered up and down between goalpost and goal-post, and the black ponies were getting more confident as they felt they had the legs of the others. The ball was hit out of a little scrimmage, and Benami and The Rabbit followed it, Faiz-Ullah only too glad to be quiet for an instant.

The blinkered black pony came up like a hawk, with two of his own side behind him, and Benami's eye glittered as he raced. The question was which pony should make way for the other, for each rider was perfectly willing to risk a fall in a good cause. The black, who had been driven nearly crazy by his blinkers, trusted to his weight and his temper; but Benami knew how to apply his weight and how to keep his temper. They met, and there was a cloud of dust. The black was lying on his side, all the breath knocked out of his body. The Rabbit was a hundred yards up the ground with the ball, and Benami was sitting down. He had slid nearly ten yards on his tail, but he had had his revenge, and sat cracking his nostrils till the black pony rose.

"That's what you get for interfering. Do you want any more?" said Benami, and he plunged into the game. Nothing was done that quarter, because Faiz-Ullah would not gallop, though Macnamara beat him whenever he could spare a second. The fall of the black pony had impressed his companions tremendously, and so the Archangels could not profit by Faiz-Ullah's bad behaviour.

But as The Maltese Cat said when "time" was called, and the four came back blowing and dripping, Faiz-Ullah ought to have been kicked all round Umballa. If he did not behave better next time The Maltese Cat promised to pull out his Arab tail by the roots and — eat it.

There was no time to talk, for the third four were ordered out.

The third quarter of a game is generally the

THE MALTESE CAT

hottest, for each side thinks that the others must be pumped; and most of the winning play in a game is made about that time.

Lutyens took over The Maltese Cat with a pat and a hug, for Lutyens valued him more than anything else in the world; Powell had Shikast, a little grey rat with no pedigree and no manners outside polo; Macnamara mounted Bamboo, the largest of the team; and Hughes Who's Who, alias The Animal. He was supposed to have Australian blood in his veins, but he looked like a clothes-horse, and you could whack his legs with an iron crowbar without hurting him.

They went out to meet the very flower of the Archangels' team; and when Who's Who saw their elegantly booted legs and their beautiful satin skins, he grinned a grin through his light, well-worn bridle.

"My word!" said Who's Who. "We must give 'em a little football. These gentlemen need a rubbing down."

"No biting," said The Maltese Cat, warningly; for once or twice in his career Who's Who had been known to forget himself in that way.

"Who said anything about biting? I'm not playing tiddly-winks. I'm playing the game."

The Archangels came down like a wolf on the fold, for they were tired of football, and they wanted polo. They got it more and more. Just after the game began, Lutyens hit a ball that was coming towards him rapidly, and it rolled in the air, as a ball sometimes will, with the whirl of a frightened partridge. Shikast heard, but could not see it for the minute, though he looked everywhere and up into the air as The Maltese Cat had taught him. When he saw it ahead and overhead he went forward with Powell as fast as he could put foot to ground. It was then that Powell, a quiet and level-headed man, as a rule, became inspired, and played a stroke that sometimes comes off successfully after long practice. He took his stick in both hands, and, standing up in his stirrups, swiped at the ball in the air, Munipore fashion. There was one second of paralysed astonishment, and then all four sides of the ground went up in a yell of applause and delight as the ball flew true (you could see the amazed Archangels ducking in their saddles to dodge the line of flight, and looking at it with open mouths), and the regimental pipes of the Skidars squealed from the railings as long as the pipers had breath.

Shikast heard the stroke; but he heard the head of the stick fly off at the same time. Nine hundred and ninety-nine ponies out of a thousand would have gone tearing on after the ball with a useless player pulling at their heads; but Powell knew him, and he knew Powell; and the instant he felt Powell's right leg shift a trifle on the saddle-flap, he headed to the boundary, where a native officer was frantically waving a new stick. Before the shouts had ended, Powell was armed again.

Once before in his life The Maltese Cat had heard that very same stroke played off his own back, and had profited by the confusion it wrought. This time he acted on experience, and leaving Bamboo to guard the goal in case of accidents, came through the others like a flash, head and tail low — Lutyens standing up to ease him — swept on and on before the other side knew what was the matter, and nearly pitched on his head between the Archangels' goal-post as Lutyens kicked the ball in after a straight scurry of a hundred and fifty yards. If there was one thing more than another upon which The Maltese Cat prided himself, it was on this quick, streaking kind of run half across the ground. He did not believe in taking balls round the field unless you were clearly over-matched. After this they gave the Archangels five-minuted football; and an expensive fast pony hates football because it rumples his temper.

Who's Who showed himself even better than Polaris in this game. He did not permit any wriggling away, but bored joyfully into the scrimmage as if he had his nose in a feed-box and was looking for something nice. Little Shikast jumped on the ball the minute it got clear, and every time an Archangel pony followed it, he found Shikast standing over it, asking what was the matter.

"If we can live through this quarter," said The Maltese Cat, "I sha'n't care. Don't take it out of yourselves. Let them do the lathering."

So the ponies, as their riders explained afterwards, "shut-up." The Archangels kept them tied fast in front of their goal, but it cost the Archangels' ponies all that was left of their tempers; and ponies began to kick, and men began to repeat compliments, and they chopped at the legs of Who's Who, and he set his teeth and stayed where he was, and the dust stood up like a tree over the scrimmage until that hot quarter ended.

They found the ponies very excited and confident when they went to their *saises;* and The Maltese Cat had to warn them that the worst of the game was coming.

"Now *we* are all going in for the second time," said he, "and *they* are trotting out fresh ponies. You think you can gallop, but you'll find you can't; and then you'll be sorry."

"But two goals to nothing is a halter-long lead," said Kittiwynk, prancing.

"How long does it take to get a goal?" The Maltese Cat answered. "For pity's sake, don't run away with a notion that the game is half-won just because we happen to be in luck *now!*

'They'll ride you into the grand stand, if they can; you must not give 'em a chance. Follow the ball."

"Football, as usual?" said Polaris. "My hock's half as big as a nose-bag."

"Don't let them have a look at the ball, if you can help it. Now leave me alone. I must get all the rest I can before the last quarter."

He hung down his head and let all his muscles go slack, Shikast, Bamboo, and Who's Who copying his example.

"Better not watch the game," he said. "We aren't playing, and we shall only take it out of ourselves if we grow anxious. Look at the ground and pretend it's fly-time."

They did their best, but it was hard advice to follow. The hooves were drumming and the sticks were rattling all up and down the ground, and yells of applause from the English troops told that the Archangels were pressing the Skidars hard. The native soldiers behind the ponies groaned and grunted, and said things in undertones, and presently they heard a long-drawn shout and a clatter of hurrahs!

"One to the Archangels," said Shikast, without raising his head. "Time's nearly up. Oh, my sire — and *dam!*"

"Faiz-Ullah," said The Maltese Cat, "if you don't play to the last nail in your shoes this time,

I'll kick you on the ground before all the other ponies."

"I'll do my best when my time comes," said the little Arab, sturdily.

The *saises* looked at each other gravely as they rubbed their ponies' legs. This was the time when long purses began to tell, and everybody knew it. Kittiwynk and the others came back, the sweat dripping over their hooves and their tails telling sad stories.

"They're better than we are," said Shiraz. "I knew how it would be."

"Shut your big head," said The Maltese Cat; "we've one goal to the good yet."

"Yes; but it's two Arabs and two country-breds to play now," said Corks. "Faiz-Ullah, remember!" He spoke in a biting voice.

As Lutyens mounted Grey Dawn he looked at his men, and they did not look pretty. They were covered with dust and sweat in streaks. Their yellow boots were almost black, their wrists were red and lumpy, and their eyes seemed two inches deep in their heads; but the expression in the eyes was satisfactory.

"Did you take anything at tiffin?" said Lutyens; and the team shook their heads. They were too dry to talk.

"All right. The Archangels did. They are worse pumped than we are."

"They've got the better ponies," said Powell. "I sha'n't be sorry when this business is over."

That fifth quarter was a painful one in every way. Faiz-Ullah played like a little red demon, and The Rabbit seemed to be everywhere at once, and Benami rode straight at anything and everything that came in his way; while the umpires on their ponies wheeled like gulls outside the shifting game. But the Archangels had the better mounts,—they had kept their racers till late in the game,—and never allowed the Skidars to play football. They hit the ball up and down the width of the ground till Benami and the rest were outpaced. Then they went forward, and time and again Lutyens and Grey Dawn were just, and only just, able to send the ball away with a long, spitting backhander. Grey Dawn forgot that he was an Arab, and turned from grey to blue as he galloped. Indeed, he forgot too well, for he did not keep his eyes on the ground as an Arab should, but stuck out his nose and scuttled for the dear honour of the game. They had watered the ground once or twice between the quarters, and a careless waterman had emptied the last of his skinful all in one place near the Skidars' goal. It was close to the end of the play, and for the tenth time Grey Dawn was bolting after the ball, when his near hind foot slipped on the greasy mud, and he rolled over and

over, pitching Lutyens just clear of the goal-post;
and the triumphant Archangels made their goal.
Then "time" was called — two goals all; but
Lutyens had to be helped up, and Grey Dawn
rose with his near hind leg strained somewhere.

"What's the damage?" said Powell, his arm
around Lutyens.

"Collar-bone, *of* course," said Lutyens, between
his teeth.   It was the third time he had broken it
in two years, and it hurt him.

Powell and the others whistled.

"'Game's up," said Hughes.

"Hold on.   We've five good minutes yet, and
it isn't my right hand.   We'll stick it out."

"I say," said the Captain of the Archangels,
trotting up, "are you hurt, Lutyens?   We'll wait
if you care to put in a substitute.   I wish — I
mean — the fact is, you fellows deserve this game
if any team does.   'Wish we could give you a
man, or some of our ponies — or something."

"You're awfully good, but we'll play it to a
finish, I think."

The Captain of the Archangels stared for a little.
"That's not half bad," he said, and went back to
his own side, while Lutyens borrowed a scarf from
one of his native officers and made a sling of it.
Then an Archangel galloped up with a big bath-
sponge, and advised Lutyens to put it under his
armpit to ease his shoulder, and between them

they tied up his left arm scientifically; and one of the native officers leaped forward with four long glasses that fizzed and bubbled.

The team looked at Lutyens piteously, and he nodded. It was the last quarter, and nothing would matter after that. They drank out the dark golden drink, and wiped their moustaches, and things looked more hopeful.

The Maltese Cat had put his nose into the front of Lutyens' shirt and was trying to say how sorry he was.

"He knows," said Lutyens, proudly. "The beggar knows. I've played him without a bridle before now — for fun."

"It's no fun now," said Powell. "But we haven't a decent substitute."

"No," said Lutyens. "It's the last quarter, and we've got to make our goal and win. I'll trust The Cat."

"If you fall this time, you'll suffer a little," said Macnamara.

"I'll trust The Cat," said Lutyens.

"You hear that?" said The Maltese Cat, proudly, to the others. "It's worth while playing polo for ten years to have that said of you. Now then, my sons, come along. We'll kick up a little bit, just to show the Archangels this team haven't suffered."

And, sure enough, as they went on to the

63

ground, The Maltese Cat, after satisfying himself that Lutyens was home in the saddle, kicked out three or four times, and Lutyens laughed. The reins were caught up anyhow in the tips of his strapped left hand, and he never pretended to rely on them. He knew The Cat would answer to the least pressure of the leg, and by way of showing off — for his shoulder hurt him very much — he bent the little fellow in a close figure-of-eight in and out between the goal-posts. There was a roar from the native officers and men, who dearly loved a piece of *dugabashi* (horse-trick work), as they called it, and the pipes very quietly and scornfully droned out the first bars of a common bazaar tune called "Freshly Fresh and Newly New," just as a warning to the other regiments that the Skidars were fit. All the natives laughed.

"And now," said The Maltese Cat, as they took their place, "remember that this is the last quarter, and follow the ball!"

"Don't need to be told," said Who's Who.

"Let me go on. All those people on all four sides will begin to crowd in — just as they did at Malta. You'll hear people calling out, and moving forward and being pushed back; and that is going to make the Archangel ponies very unhappy. But if a ball is struck to the boundary, you go after it, and let the people get out of your way. I went over the pole of a four-in-hand once, and picked a game out of the dust by it. Back me up when I run, and follow the ball."

There was a sort of an all-round sound of sympathy and wonder as the last quarter opened, and then there began exactly what The Maltese Cat had foreseen. People crowded in close to the boundaries, and the Archangels' ponies kept looking sideways at the narrowing space. If you know how a man feels to be cramped at tennis — not because he wants to run out of the court, but because he likes to know that he can at a pinch — you will guess how ponies must feel when they are playing in a box of human beings.

" I'll bend some of those men if I can get away," said Who's Who, as he rocketed behind the ball; and Bamboo nodded without speaking. They were playing the last ounce in them, and The Maltese Cat had left the goal undefended to join them. Lutyens gave him every order that he could to bring him back, but this was the first time in his career that the little wise grey had ever played polo on his own responsibility, and he was going to make the most of it.

" What are you doing here ? " said Hughes, as The Cat crossed in front of him and rode off an Archangel.

" The Cat's in charge — mind the goal ! " shouted Lutyens, and bowing forward hit the ball

full, and followed on, forcing the Archangels towards their own goal.

"No football," said The Maltese Cat. "Keep
the ball by the boundaries and cramp 'em. Play
open order, and drive 'em to the boundaries."

Across and across the ground in big diagonals
flew the ball, and whenever it came to a flying
rush and a stroke close to the boundaries the Archangel ponies moved stiffly. They did not care to
go headlong at a wall of men and carriages, though
if the ground had been open they could have
turned on a sixpence.

"Wriggle her up the sides," said The Cat.
"Keep her close to the crowd. They hate the
carriages. Shikast, keep her up this side."

Shikast and Powell lay left and right behind
the uneasy scuffle of an open scrimmage, and
every time the ball was hit away Shikast galloped
on it at such an angle that Powell was forced to
hit it towards the boundary; and when the crowd
had been driven away from that side, Lutyens
would send the ball over to the other, and Shikast
would slide desperately after it till his friends came
down to help. It was billiards, and no football,
this time — billiards in a corner pocket; and the
cues were not well chalked.

"If they get us out in the middle of the ground
they'll walk away from us. Dribble her along the
sides," cried The Maltese Cat.

So they dribbled all along the boundary, where a pony could not come on their right-hand side; and the Archangels were furious, and the umpires had to neglect the game to shout at the people to get back, and several blundering mounted policemen tried to restore order, all close to the scrimmage, and the nerves of the Archangels' ponies stretched and broke like cobwebs.

Five or six times an Archangel hit the ball up into the middle of the ground, and each time the watchful Shikast gave Powell his chance to send it back, and after each return, when the dust had settled, men could see that the Skidars had gained a few yards.

Every now and again there were shouts of "Side! Off side!" from the spectators; but the teams were too busy to care, and the umpires had all they could do to keep their maddened ponies clear of the scuffle.

At last Lutyens missed a short easy stroke, and the Skidars had to fly back helter-skelter to protect their own goal, Shikast leading. Powell stopped the ball with a backhander when it was not fifty yards from the goal-posts, and Shikast spun round with a wrench that nearly hoisted Powell out of his saddle.

"Now's our last chance," said The Cat, wheeling like a cockchafer on a pin. "We've got to ride it out. Come along."

67

Lutyens felt the little chap take a deep breath, and, as it were, crouch under his rider. The ball was hopping towards the right-hand boundary, an Archangel riding for it with both spurs and a whip; but neither spur nor whip would make his pony stretch himself as he neared the crowd. The Maltese Cat glided under his very nose, picking up his hind legs sharp, for there was not a foot to spare between his quarters and the other pony's bit. It was as neat an exhibition as fancy figure-skating. Lutyens hit with all the strength he had left, but the stick slipped a little in his hand, and the ball flew off to the left instead of keeping close to the boundary. Who's Who was far across the ground, thinking hard as he galloped. He repeated stride for stride The Cat's manœuvres with another Archangel pony, nipping the ball away from under his bridle, and clearing his opponent by half a fraction of an inch, for Who's Who was clumsy behind. Then he drove away towards the right as The Maltese Cat came up from the left; and Bamboo held a middle course exactly between them. The three were making a sort of Government-broad-arrow-shaped attack; and there was only the Archangels' back to guard the goal; but immediately behind them were three Archangels racing all they knew, and mixed up with them was Powell sending Shikast along on what he felt was their last hope. It takes a very good man to stand up to the rush of seven crazy ponies in the last quarters of a Cup game, when men are riding with their necks for sale, and the ponies are delirious. The Archangels' back missed his stroke and pulled aside just in time to let the rush go by. Bamboo and Who's Who shortened stride to give The Cat room, and Lutyens got the goal with a clean, smooth, smacking stroke that was heard all over the field. But there was no stopping the ponies. They poured through the goal-posts in one mixed mob, winners and losers together, for the pace had been terrific. The Maltese Cat knew by experience what would happen, and, to save Lutyens, turned to the right with one last effort, that strained a back-sinew beyond hope of repair. As he did so he heard the right-hand goal-post crack as a pony cannoned into it — crack, splinter, and fall like a mast. It had been sawed three parts through in case of accidents, but it upset the pony nevertheless, and he blundered into another, who blundered into the left-hand post, and then there was confusion and dust and wood. Bamboo was lying on the ground, seeing stars; an Archangel pony rolled beside him, breathless and angry; Shikast had sat down dog-fashion to avoid falling over the others, and was sliding along on his little bobtail in a cloud of dust; and Powell was sitting on the ground, hammering with his stick and trying to cheer. All the others were shouting at the top of what was left of their voices, and the men who had been spilt were shouting too. As soon as the people saw no one was hurt, ten thousand native and English shouted and clapped and yelled, and before any one could stop them the pipers of the Skidars broke on to the ground, with all the native officers and men behind them, and marched up and down, playing a wild Northern tune called " Zakhme Bagán," and through the insolent blaring of the pipes and the high-pitched native yells you could hear the Archangels' band hammering, " For they are all jolly good fellows," and then reproachfully to the losing team, "Ooh, Kafoozalum! Kafoozalum! Kafoozalum!"

Besides all these things and many more, there was a Commander-in-chief, and an Inspector-General of Cavalry, and the principal veterinary officer of all India standing on the top of a regimental coach, yelling like school-boys; and brigadiers and colonels and commissioners, and hundreds of pretty ladies joined the chorus. But The Maltese Cat stood with his head down, wondering how many legs were left to him; and Lutyens watched the men and ponies pick themselves out of the wreck of the two goal-posts, and he patted The Maltese Cat very tenderly.

" I say," said the Captain of the Archangels, spitting a pebble out of his mouth, "will you take three thousand for that pony—as he stands?"

"No, thank you. I've an idea he's saved my life," said Lutyens, getting off and lying down at full length. Both teams were on the ground too, waving their boots in the air, and coughing and drawing deep breaths, as the *saises* ran up to take away the ponies, and an officious water-carrier sprinkled the players with dirty water till they sat up.

"My aunt!" said Powell, rubbing his back, and looking at the stumps of the goal-posts, "that was a game!"

They played it over again, every stroke of it, that night at the big dinner, when the Free-for-All Cup was filled and passed down the table, and emptied and filled again, and everybody made most eloquent speeches. About two in the morning, when there might have been some singing, a wise little, plain little, grey little head looked in through the open door.

"Hurrah! Bring him in," said the Archangels; and his *sais*, who was very happy indeed, patted The Maltese Cat on the flank, and he limped in to the blaze of light and the glittering uniforms, looking for Lutyens. He was used to messes, and men's bedrooms, and places where ponies are not usually encouraged, and in his youth had jumped on and off a mess-table for a bet. So he behaved himself very politely, and ate bread dipped in salt, and was petted all round the table, moving gingerly; and they drank his health, because he had done more to win the Cup than any man or horse on the ground.

That was glory and honour enough for the rest of his days, and The Maltese Cat did not complain much when the veterinary surgeon said that he would be no good for polo any more. When Lutyens married, his wife did not allow him to play, so he was forced to be an umpire; and his pony on these occasions was a flea-bitten grey with a neat polo-tail, lame all round, but desperately quick on his feet, and, as everybody knew, Past Pluperfect Prestissimo Player of the Game.

"BREAD UPON THE WATERS"

"BREAD UPON THE WATERS"

IF you remember my improper friend Brugglesmith, you will also bear in mind his friend Mc-
Phee, Chief Engineer of the *Breslau*, whose dinghy
Brugglesmith tried to steal. His apologies for
the performances of Brugglesmith may one day be
told in their proper place: the tale before us con-
cerns McPhee. He was never a racing engineer,
and took special pride in saying as much before
the Liverpool men; but he had a thirty-two years'
knowledge of machinery and the humours of
ships. One side of his face had been wrecked
through the bursting of a pressure-gauge in the
days when men knew less than they do now, and
his nose rose grandly out of the wreck, like a club
in a public riot. There were cuts and lumps on his
head, and he would guide your forefinger through
his short iron-grey hair and tell you how he had
come by his trade-marks. He owned all sorts of
certificates of extra-competency, and at the bottom of his cabin chest of drawers, where he kept
the photograph of his wife, were two or three
Royal Humane Society medals for saving lives at

75

sea. Professionally — it was different when crazy steerage passengers jumped overboard — professionally, McPhee does not approve of saving life at sea, and he has often told me that a new Hell awaits stokers and trimmers who sign for a strong man's pay and fall sick the second day out. He believes in throwing boots at fourth and fifth engineers when they wake him up at night with word that a bearing is red-hot, all because a lamp's glare is reflected red from the twirling metal. He believes that there are only two poets in the world; one being Robert Burns, of course, and the other Gerald Massey. When he has time for novels he reads Wilkie Collins and Charles Reade — chiefly the latter — and knows whole pages of "Very Hard Cash" by heart. In the saloon his table is next to the captain's, and he drinks only water while his engines work.

He was good to me when we first met, because I did not ask questions, and believed in Charles Reade as a most shamefully neglected author. Later he approved of my writings to the extent of one pamphlet of twenty-four pages that I wrote for Holdock, Steiner & Chase, owners of the line, when they bought some ventilating patent and fitted it to the cabins of the *Breslau*, *Spandau*, and *Koltzau*. The purser of the *Breslau* recommended me to Holdock's secretary for the job; and Holdock, who is a Wesleyan Methodist, invited me to his house, and gave me dinner with the governess when the others had finished, and placed the plans and specifications in my hand, and I wrote the pamphlet that same afternoon. It was called "Comfort in the Cabin," and brought me seven pound ten, cash down — an important sum of money in those days; and the governess, who was teaching Master John Holdock his scales, told me that Mrs. Holdock had told her to keep an eye on me, in case I went away with coats from the hat-rack. McPhee liked that pamphlet enormously, for it was composed in the Bouverie-Byzantine style, with baroque and rococo embellishments; and afterwards he introduced me to Mrs. McPhee, who succeeded Dinah in my heart; for Dinah was half a world away, and it is wholesome and antiseptic to love such a woman as Janet McPhee. They lived in a little twelve-pound house, close to the shipping. When McPhee was away Mrs. McPhee read the Lloyds column in the papers, and called on the wives of senior engineers of equal social standing. Once or twice, too, Mrs. Holdock visited Mrs. McPhee in a brougham with celluloid fittings, and I have reason to believe that, after she had played owner's wife long enough, they talked scandal. The Holdocks lived in an old-fashioned house with a big brick garden not a mile from the McPhees, for they stayed by their money as their money stayed by them; and in summer you met their brougham solemnly junketing by Theydon Bois or Loughton. But I was Mrs. McPhee's friend, for she allowed me to convoy her westward, sometimes, to theatres where she sobbed or laughed or shivered with a simple heart; and she introduced me to a new world of doctors' wives, captains' wives, and engineers' wives, whose whole talk and thought centred in and about ships and lines of ships you have never heard of. There were sailing-ships, with stewards and mahogany and maple saloons, trading to Australia, taking cargoes of consumptives and hopeless drunkards for whom a sea-voyage was recommended; there were frowzy little West African boats, full of rats and cockroaches, where men died anywhere but in their bunks; there were Brazilian boats whose cabins could be hired for merchandise, that went out loaded nearly awash; there were Zanzibar and Mauritius steamers and wonderful reconstructed boats that plied to the other side of Borneo. These were loved and known, for they earned our bread and a little butter, and we despised the big Atlantic boats, and made fun of the P. & O. and Orient liners, and swore by our respective owners — Wesleyan, Baptist, or Presbyterian, as the case might be.

I had only just come back to England when Mrs. McPhee invited me to dinner at three o'clock in the afternoon, and the notepaper was almost bridal in its scented creaminess. When I reached the house I saw that there were new curtains in the window that must have cost forty-five shillings a pair; and as Mrs. McPhee drew me into the little marble-papered hall, she looked at me keenly, and cried:

"Have ye not heard? What d' ye think o' the hat-rack?"

Now, that hat-rack was oak — thirty shillings, at least. McPhee came down-stairs with a sober foot — he steps as lightly as a cat, for all his weight, when he is at sea — and shook hands in a new and awful manner — a parody of old Holdock's style when he says good-bye to his skippers. I perceived at once that a legacy had come to him, but I held my peace, though Mrs. McPhee begged me every thirty seconds to eat a great deal and say nothing. It was rather a mad sort of meal, because McPhee and his wife took hold of hands like little children (they always do after voyages), and nodded and winked and choked and gurgled, and hardly ate a mouthful.

A female servant came in and waited; though Mrs. McPhee had told me time and again that she would thank no one to do her housework while she had her health. But this was a servant with a cap, and I saw Mrs. McPhee swell and swell under her *garance*-coloured gown. There is no small

79

free-board to Janet McPhee, nor is *garance* any
subdued tint; and with all this unexplained pride
and glory in the air I felt like watching fireworks
without knowing the festival. When the maid
had removed the cloth she brought a pineapple
that would have cost half a guinea at that season
(only McPhee has his own way of getting such
things), and a Canton china bowl of dried lichis,
and a glass plate of preserved ginger, and a small
jar of sacred and Imperial chow-chow that per-
fumed the room. McPhee gets it from a Dutch-
man in Java, and I think he doctors it with
liqueurs. But the crown of the feast was some
Madeira of the kind you can only come by if you
know the wine and the man. A little maize-
wrapped fig of clotted Madeira cigars went with
the wine, and the rest was a pale-blue smoky
silence; Janet, in her splendour, smiling on us
two, and patting McPhee's hand.

"We'll drink," said McPhee, slowly, rubbing
his chin, "to the eternal damnation o' Holdock,
Steiner & Chase."

Of course I answered "Amen," though I had made
seven pound ten shillings out of the firm. McPhee's
enemies were mine, and I was drinking his Madeira.

"Ye've heard nothing?" said Janet. "Not a
word, not a whisper?"

"Not a word, nor a whisper. On my word, I
have not."

"Tell him, Mac," said she; and that is another proof of Janet's goodness and wifely love. A smaller woman would have babbled first, but Janet is five feet nine in her stockings.

"We're rich," said McPhee. I shook hands all round.

"We're damned rich," he added. I shook hands all round a second time.

"I'll go to sea no more — unless — there's no sayin' — a private yacht, maybe — wi' a small an' handy auxiliary."

"It's not enough for *that*," said Janet. "We're fair rich — well-to-do, but no more. A new gown for church, and one for the theatre. We'll have it made west."

"How much is it?" I asked.

"Twenty-five thousand pounds." I drew a long breath. "An' I've been earnin' twenty-five an' twenty pound a month!" The last words came away with a roar, as though the wide world was conspiring to beat him down.

"All this time I'm waiting," I said. "I know nothing since last September. Was it left you?"

They laughed aloud together. "It was left," said McPhee, choking. "Ou, ay, it was left. That's vara good. Of course it was left. Janet, d' ye note that? It was left. Now if you'd put *that* in your pamphlet it would have been vara jocose. It *was* left." He slapped his thigh and roared till the wine quivered in the decanter.

The Scotch are a great people, but they are apt to hang over a joke too long, particularly when no one can see the point but themselves.

"When I rewrite my pamphlet I'll put it in, Mc-Phee. Only I must know something more first."

McPhee thought for the length of half a cigar, while Janet caught my eye and led it round the room to one new thing after another — the new vine-pattern carpet, the new chiming rustic clock between the models of the Colombo outrigger-boats, the new inlaid sideboard with a purple cut-glass flower-stand, the fender of gilt and brass, and last, the new black-and-gold piano.

"In October o' last year the Board sacked me," began McPhee. "In October o' last year the *Breslau* came in for winter overhaul. She'd been runnin' eight months — two hunder an' forty days — an' I was three days makin' up my in-dents, when she went to dry-dock. All told, mark you, it was this side o' three hunder pound — to be preceese, two hunder an' eighty-six pound four shillings. There's not another man could ha' nursed the *Breslau* for eight months to that tune. Never again — never again! They may send their boats to the bottom, for aught I care."

"There's no need," said Janet, softly. "We're done wi' Holdock, Steiner & Chase."

"It's irritatin', Janet, it's just irritatin'. I ha' been justified from first to last, as the world knows, but — but I canna forgie 'em. Ay, wisdom is justified o' her children; an' any other man than me wad ha' made the indent eight hunder. Hay was our skipper — ye'll have met him. They shifted him to the *Torgau*, an' bade me wait for the *Breslau* under young Bannister. Ye'll obsairve there'd been a new election on the Board. I heard the shares were sellin' hither an' yon, an' the major part of the Board was new to me. The old Board would ne'er ha' done it. They trusted me. But the new Board were all for reorganisation. Young Steiner — Steiner's son — the Jew, was at the bottom of it, an' they did not think it worth their while to send me word. The first *I* knew — an' I was Chief Engineer — was the notice of the line's winter sailin's, an' the *Breslau* timed for sixteen days between port an' port! Sixteen days, man! She's a good boat, but eighteen is her summer time, mark you. Sixteen was sheer flytin', kitin' nonsense, an' so I told young Bannister.

"'We've got to make it,' he said. 'Ye should not ha' sent in a three hunder pound indent.'

"'Do they look for their boats to be run on air?' I said. 'The Board's daft.'

"'E'en tell 'em so,' he says. 'I'm a married man, an' my fourth's on the ways now, she says.'"

"A boy — wi' red hair," Janet put in. Her own

hair is the splendid red-gold that goes with a creamy complexion.

"My word, I was an angry man that day! Forbye I was fond o' the old *Breslau*, I looked for a little consideration from the Board after twenty years' service. There was Board-meetin' on Wednesday, an' I slept overnight in the engine-room, takin' figures to support my case. Well, I put it fair an' square before them all. 'Gentlemen,' I said, 'I've run the *Breslau* eight seasons, an' I believe there's no fault to find wi' my wark. But if ye haud to this'——I waggled the advertisement at 'em —'this that *I've* never heard of it till I read it at breakfast, I do assure you on my professional reputation, she can never do it. That is to say, she can for a while, but at a risk no thinkin' man would run.'

"'What the deil d' ye suppose we pass your indents for?' says old Holdock. 'Man, we're spendin' money like watter.'

"'I'll leave it in the Board's hands,' I said, 'if two hunder an' eighty-seven pound is anything beyond right an' reason for eight months.' I might ha' saved my breath, for the Board was new since the last election, an' there they sat, the damned deevidend-huntin' ship-chandlers, deaf as the adders o' Scripture.

"'We must keep faith wi' the public,' said young Steiner.

"'Keep faith wi' the *Breslau*, then,' I said. 'She's served you well, an' your father before you. She'll need her bottom restiffenin', an' new bed-plates, an' turnin' out the forward boilers, an' re-turnin' all three cylinders, an' refacin' all guides, to begin with. It's a three months' job.'

"'Because one employé is afraid?' says young Steiner. 'Maybe a piano in the Chief Engineer's cabin would be more to the point.'

"I crushed my cap in my hands, an' thanked God we'd no bairns an' a bit put by.

"'Understand, gentlemen,' I said. 'If the *Breslau* is made a sixteen-day boat, ye'll find another engineer.'

"'Bannister makes no objection,' said Holdock.

"'I'm speakin' for myself,' I said. 'Bannister has bairns.' An' then I lost my temper. 'Ye can run her into Hell an' out again if ye pay pilotage,' I said, 'but ye run without me.'

"'That's insolence,' said young Steiner.

"'At your pleasure,' I said, turnin' to go.

"'Ye can consider yourself dismissed. We must preserve discipline among our employés,' said old Holdock, an' he looked round to see that the Board was with him. They knew nothin'— God forgie 'em — an' they nodded me out o' the line after twenty years — after twenty years.

"I went out an' sat down by the hall porter to get my wits again. I'm thinkin' I swore at the

Board. Then auld McRimmon — o' McNaughten & McRimmon — came oot o' his office, that's on the same floor, an' looked at me, proppin' up one eyelid wi' his forefinger. Ye know they call him the Blind Deevil, forbye he's onythin' but blind, an' no deevil in his dealin's wi' me — McRimmon o' the Black Bird Line.

" ' What's here, Mister McPhee ? ' said he.

" I was past prayin' for by then. 'A Chief Engineer sacked after twenty years' service because he'll not risk the *Breslau* on the new timin', an' be damned to ye, McRimmon,' I said.

" The auld man sucked in his lips an' whistled. ' Ah,' said he, ' the new timin'. I see ! ' He doddered into the Board-room I'd just left, an' the Dandie-dog that is just his blind man's leader stayed wi' me. *That* was providential. In a minute he was back again. ' Ye've cast your bread on the watter, McPhee, an' be damned to you,' he says. ' Whaur's my dog ? My word, is he on your knee ? There's more discernment in a dog than a Jew. What garred ye curse your Board, McPhee ? It's expensive.'

" ' They'll pay more for the *Breslau*,' I said. ' Get off my knee, ye smotherin' beast.'

" ' Bearin's hot, eh ? ' said McRimmon. ' It's thirty year since a man daur curse me to my face. Time was I'd ha' cast ye doon the stairway for that.'

" ' Forgie 's all ! ' I said. He was wearin' to

eighty, as I knew. 'I was wrong, McRimmon; but when a man's shown the door for doin' his plain duty, he's not always ceevil.'

"'So I hear,' says McRimmon. 'Ha' ye ony objection to a tramp freighter? It's only fifteen a month, but they say the Blind Deevil feeds a man better than others. She's my *Kite*. Come ben. Ye can thank Dandie, here. I'm no used to thanks. An' noo,' says he, 'what possessed ye to throw up your berth wi' Holdock?'

"'The new timin',' said I. 'The *Breslau* will not stand it.'

"'Hoot, oot,' said he. 'Ye might ha' crammed her a little — enough to show ye were drivin' her — an' brought her in twa days behind. What's easier than to say ye slowed for bearin's, eh? All my men do it, and — I believe 'em.'

"'McRimmon,' says I, 'what's her virginity to a lassie?'

"He puckered his dry face an' twisted in his chair. 'The warld an' a',' says he. 'My God, the vara warld an' a'! But what ha' you or me to do wi' virginity, this late along?'

"'This,' I said. 'There's just one thing that each one of us in his trade or profession will *not* do for ony consideration whatever. If I run to time I run to time, barrin' always the risks o' the high seas. Less than that, under God, I have not done. More than that, by God, I will not do!

There's no trick o' the trade I'm not acquaint
wi'—'

" ' So I've heard,' says McRimmon, dry as a
biscuit.

" ' But yon matter o' fair runnin' 's just my She-
kinah, ye'll understand. I daurna tamper wi' *that*.
Nursing weak engines is fair craftsmanship; but
what the Board ask is cheatin', wi' the risk o'
manslaughter addeetional.' Ye'll note I know my
business.

" There was some more talk, an' next week I
went aboard the *Kite*, twenty-five hunder ton, simple compound, a Black Bird tramp. The deeper
she rode, the better she'd steam. I've snapped as
much as eleven out of her, but eight point three
was her fair normal. Good food forward an' better aft, all indents passed wi'out marginal remarks,
the best coal, new donkeys, an' good crews.
There was nothin' the old man would not do, except paint. That was his deeficulty. Ye could
no more draw paint than his last teeth from him.
He'd come down to dock, an' his boats a scandal
all along the watter, an' he'd whine an' cry an'
say they looked all he could desire. Every owner
has his *non plus ultra*, I've obsairved. Paint was
McRimmon's. But you could get round his
engines without riskin' your life; an', for all his
blindness, I've seen him reject five flawed inter-
mediates, one after the other, on a nod from me;

an' his cattle-fittin's were guaranteed for North Atlantic winter weather. Ye ken what *that* means? McRimmon an' the Black Bird Line, God bless him!

"Oh, I forgot to say she would lie down an' fill her forward deck green, an' snore away into a twenty-knot gale forty-five to the minute, three an' a half knots an hour, the engines runnin' sweet an' true as a bairn breathin' in its sleep. Bell was skipper; an' forbye there's no love lost between crews an' owners, we were fond o' the auld Blind Deevil an' his dog, an' I'm thinkin' he liked us. He was worth the windy side o' twa million sterlin', an' no friend to his own blood-kin. Money's an awfu' thing — overmuch — for a lonely man.

"I'd taken her out twice, there an' back again, when word came o' the *Breslau's* breakdown, just as I prophesied. Calder was her engineer — he's not fit to run a tug down the Solent — an' he fairly lifted the engines off the bed-plates, an' they fell down in heaps, by what I heard. So she filled from the after stuffin'-box to the after bulkhead, an' lay star-gazing, with seventy-nine squealin' passengers in the saloon, till the *Camaralzaman* o' Ramsey & Gold's Cartagena line gave her a tow to the tune o' five thousand seven hunder an' forty pound, wi' costs in the Admiralty Court. She was helpless, ye'll understand, an' in no case to meet ony weather. Five thousand seven hunder an' forty pounds, *with* costs, an' exclusive o' new engines! They'd ha' done better to ha' kept me — on the old timin'.

"But, even so, the new Board were all for re-trenchment. Young Steiner, the Jew, was at the bottom of it. They sacked men right an' left, that would not eat the dirt the Board gave 'em. They cut down repairs; they fed crews wi' leavin's an' scrapin's; an', reversin' McRimmon's practice, they hid their defeeciencies wi' paint an' cheap gildin'. *Quem Deus vult perrdere prrius dementat,* ye remember.

"In January we went to dry-dock, an' in the next dock lay the *Grotkau,* their big freighter that was the *Dolabella* o' Piegan, Piegan & Walsh's line in '84 — a Clyde-built iron boat, a flat-bottomed, pigeon-breasted, under-engined, bull-nosed bitch of a five-thousand-ton freighter, that would neither steer, nor steam, nor stop when ye asked her. Whiles she'd attend to her helm, whiles she'd take charge, whiles she'd wait to scratch herself, an' whiles she'd buttock into a dock-head. But Holdock & Steiner had bought her cheap, an' painted her all over like the Hoor o' Babylon, an' we called her the *Hoor* for short." (By the way, McPhee kept to that name throughout the rest of his tale; so you must read accordingly.) "I went to see young Bannister — he had to take what the Board gave him, an' he an' Calder were shifted together from the *Breslau* to this abortion — an' talkin' to him I went into the dock under her. Her plates were pitted till the men that were paint, paint, paintin' her laughed at it. But the warst was at the last. She'd a great clumsy iron twelve-foot Thresher propeller — Aitcheson designed the *Kite's* — an' just on the tail o' the shaft, behind the boss, was a red weepin' crack ye could ha' put a penknife to. Man, it was an awfu' crack!

" 'When d' ye ship a new tail-shaft?' I said to Bannister.

" He knew what I meant. 'Oh, yon's a superfeecial flaw,' says he, not lookin' at me.

" 'Superfeecial Gehenna!' I said. 'Ye'll not take her oot wi' a solution o' continuity that like.'

" 'They'll putty it up this evening,' he said. 'I'm a married man, an'— ye used to know the Board.'

" I e'en said what was gied me in that hour. Ye know how a dry-dock echoes. I saw young Steiner standin' listenin' above me, an', man, he used language provocative of a breach o' the peace. I was a spy an' a disgraced employé, an' a corrupter o' young Bannister's morals, an' he'd prosecute me for libel. He went away when I ran up the steps — I'd ha' thrown him into the dock if I'd caught him — an' there I met McRimmon, wi' Dandie pullin' on the chain, guidin' the auld man among the railway lines.

"'McPhee,' said he, 'ye're no paid to fight Holdock, Steiner, Chase & Company, Limited, when ye meet. What's wrong between you?'

"'No more than a tail-shaft rotten as a kail-stump. For ony sakes go an' look, McRimmon. It's a comedietta.'

"'I'm feared o' yon conversational Hebrew,' said he. 'Whaur's the flaw, an' what like?'

"'A seven-inch crack just behind the boss. There's no power on earth will fend it just jarrin' off.'

"'When?'

"'That's beyon' my knowledge,' I said.

"'So it is; so it is,' said McRimmon. 'We've all oor leemitations. Ye're certain it was a crack?'

"'Man, it's a crevasse,' I said, for there were no words to describe the magnitude of it. 'An' young Bannister's sayin' it's no more than a superfeecial flaw!'

"'Weell, I tak' it oor business is to mind oor business. If ye've ony friends aboard her, McPhee, why not bid them to a bit dinner at Radley's?'

"'I was thinkin' o' tea in the cuddy,' I said. 'Engineers o' tramp freighters cannot afford hotel prices.'

"'Na! na!' says the auld man, whimperin'. 'Not the cuddy. They'll laugh at my *Kite*, for she's no plastered with paint like the *Hoor*. Bid them to

Radley's, McPhee, an' send me the bill. Thank Dandie, here, man. I'm no used to thanks.' Then he turned him round. (I was just thinkin' the vara same thing.) 'Mister McPhee,' said he, 'this is *not* senile dementia.'

"'Preserve 's!' I said, clean jumped oot o' my-sel'. 'I was but thinkin' you're fey, McRimmon.'

"Dod, the auld deevil laughed till he nigh sat down on Dandie. 'Send me the bill,' says he. 'I'm long past champagne, but tell me how it tastes the morn.'

"Bell an' I bid young Bannister an' Calder to dinner at Radley's. They'll have no laughin' an' singin' there, but we took a private room — like yacht-owners fra' Cowes."

McPhee grinned all over, and lay back to think.

"And then?" said I.

"We were no drunk in ony preceese sense o' the word, but Radley's showed me the dead men. There were six magnums o' dry champagne an' maybe a bottle o' whisky."

"Do you mean to tell me that you four got away with a magnum and a half apiece, besides whisky?" I demanded.

McPhee looked down upon me from between his shoulders with toleration.

"Man, we were not settin' down to drink," he said. "They no more than made us wutty. To be sure, young Bannister laid his head on the

table an' greeted like a bairn, an' Calder was all
for callin' on Steiner at two in the morn an' paint-
ing him galley-green; but they'd been drinkin'
the afternoon. Lord, how they twa cursed the
Board, an' the *Grotkau*, an' the tail-shaft, an' the
engines, an' a'! They didna talk o' superfeecial
flaws that night. I mind young Bannister an'
Calder shakin' hands on a bond to be revenged on
the Board at ony reasonable cost this side o' losing
their certificates. Now mark ye how false economy ruins business. The Board fed them like
swine (I have good reason to know it), an' I've
obsairved wi' my ain people that if ye touch his
stomach ye wauken the deil in a Scot. Men will
tak' a dredger across the Atlantic if they're well
fed, an' fetch her somewhere on the broadside o'
the Americas; but bad food's bad service the
warld over.

"The bill went to McRimmon, an' he said no
more to me till the week-end, when I was at him
for more paint, for we'd heard the *Kite* was char-
tered Liverpool-side.

"'Bide whaur ye're put,' said the Blind Deevil.
'Man, do ye wash in champagne? The *Kite's* no
leavin' here till I gie the order, an'—how am I
to waste paint on her, wi' the *Lammergeyer* docked
for who knows how long an' a'?'

"She was our big freighter—McIntyre was
engineer—an' I knew she'd come from overhaul

94

not three months. That morn I met McRimmon's head-clerk — ye'll not know him — fair bitin' his nails off wi' mortification.

"'The auld man's gone gyte,' says he. 'He's withdrawn the *Lammergeyer*.'

"'Maybe he has reasons,' says I.

"'Reasons! He's daft!'

"'He'll no be daft till he begins to paint,' I said.

"'That's just what he's done — an' South American freights higher than we'll live to see them again. He's laid her up to paint her — to paint her — to paint her!' says the little clerk, dancin' like a hen on a hot plate. 'Five thousand ton o' potential freight rottin' in dry-dock, man; an' he dolin' the paint out in quarter-pound-tins, for it cuts him to the heart, mad though he is. An' the *Grotkau* — the *Grotkau* of all conceivable bottoms — soaking up every pound that should be ours at Liverpool!'

"I was staggered wi' this folly — considerin' the dinner at Radley's in connection wi' the same.

"'Ye may well stare, McPhee,' says the head-clerk. 'There's engines, an' rollin' stock, an' iron bridges — d' ye know what freights are noo? — an' pianos, an' millinery, an' fancy Brazil cargo o' every species pourin' into the *Grotkau* — the *Grotkau* o' the Jerusalem firm — an' the *Lammergeyer's* bein' painted!'

"Losh, I thought he'd drop dead wi' the fits.

"I could say no more than 'Obey orders, if ye break owners,' but on the *Kite* we believed Mc-Rimmon was mad; an' McIntyre of the *Lammer-geyer* was for lockin' him up by some patent legal process he'd found in a book o' maritime law. An' a' that week South American freights rose an' rose. It was sinfu'!

"Syne Bell got orders to tak' the *Kite* round to Liverpool in water-ballast, an' McRimmon came to bid 's good-bye, yammerin' an' whinin' o'er the acres o' paint he'd lavished on the *Lammergeyer*.

"'I look to you to retrieve it,' says he. 'I look to you to reimburse me! 'Fore God, why are ye not cast off? Are ye dawdlin' in dock for a purpose?'

"'What odds, McRimmon?' says Bell. 'We'll be a day behind the fair at Liverpool. The *Grot-kau's* got all the freight that might ha' been ours an' the *Lammergeyer's.*' McRimmon laughed an' chuckled — the pairfect eemage o' senile demen-tia. Ye ken his eyebrows wark up an' down like a gorilla's.

"'Ye're under sealed orders,' said he, tee-heein' an' scratchin' himself. 'Yon's they' — to be opened *seriatim.*

"Says Bell, shufflin' the envelopes when the auld man had gone ashore: 'We're to creep round a' the south coast, standin' in for orders — this weather, too. There's no question o' his lunacy now.'

"Well, we buttocked the auld *Kite* along — vara bad weather we made — standin' in all alongside for telegraphic orders, which are the curse o' skippers. Syne we made over to Holyhead, an' Bell opened the last envelope for the last instructions. I was wi' him in the cuddy, an' he threw it over to me, cryin': 'Did ye ever know the like, Mac?'

"I'll no say what McRimmon had written, but he was far from mad. There was a sou'wester brewin' when we made the mouth o' the Mersey, a bitter cold morn wi' a grey-green sea an' a grey-green sky — Liverpool weather, as they say; an' there we lay choppin', an' the crew swore. Ye canna keep secrets aboard ship. They thought McRimmon was mad, too.

"Syne we saw the *Grotkau* rollin' oot on the top o' flood, deep an' double deep, wi' her new-painted funnel an' her new-painted boats an' a'. She looked her name, an', moreover, she coughed like it. Calder tauld me at Radley's what ailed his engines, but my own ear would ha' told me twa mile awa', by the beat o' them. Round we came, plungin' an' squatterin' in her wake, an' the wind cut wi' good promise o' more to come. By six it blew hard but clear, an' before the middle watch it was a sou'wester in airnest.

"'She'll edge into Ireland, this gait,' says Bell.

I was with him on the bridge, watchin' the *Grotkau's* port light. Ye canna see green so far as red, or we'd ha' kept to leeward. We'd no passengers to consider, an' (all eyes being on the *Grotkau*) we fair walked into a liner rampin' home to Liverpool. Or, to be preceese, Bell no more than twisted the *Kite* oot from under her bows, an' there was a little damnin' betwix' the twa bridges. Noo a passenger"— McPhee regarded me benignantly —"wad ha' told the papers that as soon as he got to the Customs. We stuck to the *Grotkau's* tail that night an' the next twa days — she slowed down to five knot by my reckonin' — an' we lapped along the weary way to the Fastnet."

"But you don't go by the Fastnet to get to any South American port, do you?" I said.

"*We* do not. We prefer to go as direct as may be. But we were followin' the *Grotkau*, an' she'd no walk into that gale for ony consideration. Knowin' what I did to her discredit, I couldna blame young Bannister. It was warkin' up to a North Atlantic winter gale, snow an' sleet an' a perishin' wind. Eh, it was like the Deil walkin' abroad o' the surface o' the deep, whuppin' off the top o' the waves before he made up his mind. They'd bore up against it so far, but the minute she was clear o' the Skelligs she fair tucked up her skirts an' ran for it by Dunmore Head. Wow, she rolled!

" ' She'll be makin' Smerwick,' says Bell.

" ' She'd ha' tried for Ventry by noo if she meant that,' I said.

" ' They'll roll the funnel oot o' her, this gait,' says Bell. ' Why canna Bannister keep her head to sea ? '

" ' It's the tail-shaft. Ony rollin' 's better than pitchin' wi' superfeecial cracks in the tail-shaft. Calder knows that much,' I said.

" ' It's ill wark retreevin' steamers this weather,' said Bell. His beard and whiskers were frozen to his oilskin, an' the spray was white on the weather side of him. Pairfect North Atlantic winter weather !

" One by one the sea raxed away our three boats, an' the davits were crumpled like ram's horns.

" ' Yon's bad,' said Bell, at the last. ' Ye canna pass a hawser wi'oot a boat.' Bell was a vara judeecious man—for an Aberdonian.

" I'm not one that fashes himself for eventualities outside the engine-room, so I e'en slipped down betwixt waves to see how the *Kite* fared. Man, she's the best-geared boat of her class that ever left Clyde ! Kinloch, my second, knew her as well as I did. I found him dryin' his socks on the main-steam, an' combin' his whiskers wi' the comb Janet gied me last year, for the warld an' a' as though we were in port. I tried the feed, speered into the stoke-hole, thumbed all bearin's, spat on the thrust for luck, gied 'em my blessin', an' took Kinloch's socks before I went up to the bridge again.

"Then Bell handed me the wheel, an' went below to warm himself. When he came up my gloves were frozen to the spokes an' the ice clicked over my eyelids. Pairfect North Atlantic winter weather, as I was sayin'.

"The gale blew out by night, but we lay in smotherin' cross-seas that made the auld *Kite* chatter from stem to stern. I slowed to thirty-four, I mind — no, thirty-seven. There was a long swell the morn, an' the *Grotkau* was headin' into it west awa'.

"'She'll win to Rio yet, tail-shaft or no tail-shaft,' says Bell.

"'Last night shook her,' I said. 'She'll jar it off yet, mark my word.'

"We were then, maybe, a hunder an' fifty mile west-sou'west o' Slyne Head, by dead reckonin'. Next day we made a hunder an' thirty — ye'll note we were not racin'-boats — an' the day after a hunder an' sixty-one, an' that made us, we'll say, Eighteen an' a bittock west, an' maybe Fifty-one an' a bittock north, crossin' all the North Atlantic liner lanes on the long slant, always in sight o' the *Grotkau*, creepin' up by night an' fallin' awa' by day. After the gale it was cold weather wi' dark nights.

"I was in the engine-room on Friday night, just before the middle watch, when Bell whustled down the tube: 'She's done it'; an' up I came.

"The *Grotkau* was just a fair distance south, an' one by one she ran up the three red lights in a vertical line — the sign of a steamer not under control.

"'Yon's a tow for us,' said Bell, lickin' his chops. 'She'll be worth more than the *Breslau*. We'll go down to her, McPhee!'

"'Bide a while,' I said. 'The seas fair throng wi' ships here.'

"'Reason why,' said Bell. 'It's a fortune gaun beggin'. What d' ye think, man?'

"'Gie her till daylight. She knows we're here. If Bannister needs help he'll loose a rocket.'

"'Wha told ye Bannister's need? We'll ha' some rag-an'-bone tramp snappin' her up under oor nose,' said he; an' he put the wheel over. We were goin' slow.

"'Bannister wad like better to go home on a liner an' eat in the saloon. Mind ye what they said o' Holdock & Steiner's food that night at Radley's? Keep her awa', man — keep her awa'. A tow's a tow, but a derelict's big salvage.'

"'E-eh!' said Bell. 'Yon's an inshot o' yours, Mac. I love ye like a brother. We'll bide whaur we are till daylight'; an' he kept her awa'.

"Syne up went a rocket forward, an' twa on the bridge, an' a blue light aft. Syne a tar-barrel forward again.

"'She's sinkin',' said Bell. 'It's all gaun, an' I'll get no more than a pair o' night-glasses for pickin' up young Bannister — the fool!'

"'Fair an' soft again,' I said. 'She's signallin' to the south of us. Bannister knows as well as I that one rocket would bring the *Breslau*. He'll no be wastin' fireworks for nothin'. Hear her ca'!'

"The *Grotkau* whustled an' whustled for five minutes, an' then there were more fireworks — a regular exhibeetion.

"'That's no for men in the regular trade,' says Bell. 'Ye're right, Mac. That's for a cuddy full o' passengers.' He blinked through the night-glasses when it lay a bit thick to southward.

"'What d' ye make of it?' I said.

"'Liner,' he says. 'Yon's her rocket. Ou, ay; they've waukened the gold-strapped skipper, an'— noo they've waukened the passengers. They're turnin' on the electrics, cabin by cabin. Yon's anither rocket! They're comin' up to help the perishin' in deep watters.'

"'Gie me the glass,' I said. But Bell danced on the bridge, clean dementit. 'Mails — mails — mails!' said he. 'Under contract wi' the Government for the due conveyance o' the mails; an' as such, Mac, ye'll note, she may rescue life at

sea, but she canna tow!—she canna tow! Yon's
her night-signal. She'll be up in half an hour!'

"'Gowk!' I said, 'an' we blazin' here wi' all
oor lights. Oh, Bell, ye're a fool!'

"He tumbled off the bridge forward, an' I tumbled aft, an' before ye could wink our lights were
oot, the engine-room hatch was covered, an' we
lay pitch-dark, watchin' the lights o' the liner come
up that the *Grotkau'd* been signallin' to. Twenty
knot an hour she came, every cabin lighted, an'
her boats swung awa'. It was grandly done, an'
in the inside of an hour. She stopped like Mrs.
Holdock's machine; down went the gangway,
down went the boats, an' in ten minutes we heard
the passengers cheerin', an' awa' she fled.

"'They'll tell o' this all the days they live,' said
Bell. 'A rescue at sea by night, as pretty as a
play. Young Bannister an' Calder will be drinkin'
in the saloon, an' six months hence the Board o'
Trade 'll gie the skipper a pair o' binoculars. It's
vara philanthropic all round.'

"We lay by till day—ye may think we
waited for it wi' sore eyes—an' there sat the *Grotkau,* her nose a bit cocked, just leerin' at us. She
looked pairfectly ridiculous.

"'She'll be fillin' aft,' says Bell; 'for why is she
down by the stern? The tail-shaft's punched a
hole in her, an'—we've no boats. There's three
hunder thousand pound sterlin', at a conservative

estimate, droonin' before our eyes. What's to do?'
An' his bearin's got hot again in a minute: he
was an incontinent man.

"'Run her as near as ye daur,' I said. 'Gie
me a jacket an' a life-line, an' I'll swum for it.'
There was a big lump of a sea, an' it was cold in
the wind — vara cold; but they'd gone overside
like passengers, young Bannister an' Calder an' a',
leaving the gangway down on the lee-side. It
would ha' been a flyin' in the face o' manifest Providence to overlook the invitation. We were within
fifty yards o' her while Kinloch was garmin' me all
over wi' oil behind the galley; an' as we ran past
I went outboard for the salvage o' three hunder
thousand pound. Man, it was perishin' cold, but
I'd done my job judgmatically, an' came scrapin
all along her side slap on to the lower gratin' o' the
gangway. No one more astonished than me, I assure ye. Before I'd caught my breath I'd skinned
both my knees on the gratin', an' was climbin' up
before she rolled again. I made my line fast to
the rail, an' squattered aft to young Bannister's
cabin, whaur I dried me wi' everything in his bunk,
an' put on every conceivable sort o' rig I found till
the blood was circulatin'. Three pair drawers, I
mind I found — to begin upon — an' I needed
them all. It was the coldest cold I remember in
all my experience.

"Syne I went aft to the engine-room. The

Grotkau sat on her own tail, as they say. She was
vara short-shafted, an' her gear was all aft. There
was four or five foot o' watter in the engine-room
slummockin' to an' fro, black an' greasy; maybe
there was six foot. The stoke-hold doors were
screwed home, an' the stoke-hold was tight enough,
but for a minute the mess in the engine-room de-
ceived me. Only for a minute, though, an' that
was because I was not, in a manner o' speakin', as
calm as ordinar'. I looked again to mak' sure.
'Twas just black wi' bilge : dead-watter that must
ha' come in fortuitously, ye ken."

"McPhee, I'm only a passenger," I said, "but
you don't persuade me that six foot o' water can
come into an engine-room fortuitously."

"Who's tryin' to persuade one way or the
other?" McPhee retorted. "I'm statin' the facts
o' the case — the simple, natural facts. Six or
seven foot o' dead-watter in the engine-room is a
vara depressin' sight if ye think there's like to be
more comin'; but I did not consider that such was
likely, an' so, ye'll note, I was not depressed."

"That's all very well, but I want to know about
the water," I said.

"I've told ye. There was six feet or more
there, wi' Calder's cap floatin' on top."

"Where did it come from?"

"Weel, in the confusion o' things after the propeller had dropped off an' the engines were racin'

an' a', it's vara possible that Calder might ha' lost it off his head an' no troubled himself to pick it up again. I remember seein' that cap on him at Southampton."

"I don't want to know about the cap. I'm asking where the water came from and what it was doing there, and why you were so certain that it wasn't a leak, McPhee?"

"For good reason — for good an' sufficient reason."

"Give it to me, then."

"Weel, it's a reason that does not properly concern myself only. To be preceese, I'm of opinion that it was due, the watter, in part to an error o' judgment in another man. We can a' mak' mistakes."

"Oh, I beg your pardon!"

"I got me to the rail again, an', 'What's wrang?' said Bell, hailin'.

"'She'll do,' I said. 'Send 's o'er a hawser, an' a man to steer. I'll pull him in by the life-line.'

"I could see heads bobbin' back an' forth, an' a whuff or two o' strong words. Then Bell said: 'They'll not trust themselves — one of 'em — in this watter — except Kinloch, an' I'll no spare him.'

"'The more salvage to me, then,' I said. 'I'll make shift *solo*.'

"Says one dock-rat, at this: 'D' ye think she's safe?'

"'I'll guarantee ye nothing,' I said, 'except maybe a hammerin' for keepin' me this long.'

"Then he sings out: 'There's no more than one life-belt, an' they canna find it, or I'd come.'

"'Throw him over, the Jezebel,' I said, for I was oot o' patience; an' they took haud o' that volunteer before he knew what was in store, an' hove him over, in the bight of my life-line. So I e'en hauled him upon the sag of it, hand over fist — a vara welcome recruit when I'd tilted the salt watter oot of him: for, by the way, he couldna swim.

"Syne they bent a twa-inch rope to the life-line, an' a hawser to that, an' I led the rope o'er the drum of a hand-winch forward, an' we sweated the hawser inboard an' made it fast to the *Grotkau's* bitts.

"Bell brought the *Kite* so close I feared she'd roll in an' do the *Grotkau's* plates a mischief. He hove anither life-line to me, an' went astern, an' we had all the weary winch work to do again wi' a second hawser. For all that, Bell was right: we'd a long tow before us, an' though Providence had helped us that far, there was no sense in leavin' too much to its keepin'. When the second hawser was fast, I was wet wi' sweat, an' I cried Bell to tak' up his slack an' go home. The other man was by way o' helpin' the work wi' askin' for drinks, but I e'en told him he must hand reef an'

steer, beginnin' with steerin', for I was goin' to
turn in. He steered — oh, ay, he steered, in a
manner o' speakin'. At the least, he grippit the
spokes an' twiddled 'em an' looked wise, but I
doubt if the *Hoor* ever felt it. I turned in there
an' then, to young Bannister's bunk, an' slept past
expression. I waukened ragin' wi' hunger, a fair
lump o' sea runnin', the *Kite* snorin' awa' four
knots an hour; an' the *Grotkau* slappin' her nose
under, an' yawnin' an' standin' over at discretion.
She was a most disgracefu' tow. But the shameful thing of all was the food. I raxed me a meal
fra' galley-shelves an' pantries an' lazareetes an'
cubby-holes that I would not ha' gied to the mate
of a Cardiff collier; an' ye ken we say a Cardiff
mate will eat clinkers to save waste. I'm sayin'
it was simply vile! The crew had written what
they thought of it on the new paint o' the fo'c'sle,
but I had not a decent soul wi' me to complain
on. There was nothin' for me to do save watch
the hawsers an' the *Kite's* tail squatterin' down in
white watter when she lifted to a sea; so I got
steam on the after donkey-pump, an' pumped oot
the engine-room. There's no sense in leavin'
watter loose in a ship. When she was dry, I
went doun the shaft-tunnel, an' found she was
leakin' a little through the stuffin'-box, but nothin'
to make wark. The propeller had e'en jarred off,
as I knew it must, an' Calder had been waitin' for

it to go wi' his hand on the gear. He told me as much when I met him ashore. There was nothin' started or strained. It had just slipped awa' to the bed o' the Atlantic as easy as a man dyin' wi' due warnin' — a most providential business for all concerned. Syne I took stock o' the *Grotkau's* upper works. Her boats had been smashed on the davits, an' here an' there was the rail missin', an' a ventilator or two had fetched awa', an' the bridge-rails were bent by the seas; but her hatches were tight, an' she'd taken no sort o' harm. Dod, I came to hate her like a human bein', for I was eight weary days aboard, starvin' — ay, starvin' — within a cable's length o' plenty. All day I laid in the bunk reading the 'Woman-Hater,' the grandest book Charlie Reade ever wrote, an' pickin' a toothful here an' there. It was weary, weary work. Eight days, man, I was aboard the *Grotkau*, an' not one full meal did I make. Sma' blame her crew would not stay by her. The other man? Oh, I warked him wi' a vengeance to keep him warm.

"It came on to blow when we fetched soundin's, an' that kept me standin' by the hawsers, lashed to the capstan, breathin' 'twixt green seas. I near died o' cauld an' hunger, for the *Grotkau* towed like a barge, an' Bell howkit her along through or over. It was vara thick up-Channel, too. We were standin' in to make some sort o' light, an' we near walked over twa three fishin'-boats, an' they cried us we were overclose to Falmouth. Then we were near cut down by a drunken foreign fruiter that was blunderin' between us an' the shore, an' it got thicker an' thicker that night, an' I could feel by the tow Bell did not know whaur he was. Losh, we knew in the morn, for the wind blew the fog oot like a candle, an' the sun came clear; an' as surely as McRimmon gied me my cheque, the shadow o' the Eddystone lay across our tow-rope! We were that near — ay, we were that near! Bell fetched the *Kite* round with the jerk that came close to tearin' the bitts out o' the *Grotkau*, an' I mind I thanked my Maker in young Bannister's cabin when we were inside Plymouth breakwater.

" The first to come aboard was McRimmon, wi' Dandie. Did I tell you our orders were to take anything we found into Plymouth? The auld deil had just come down overnight, puttin' two an' two together from what Calder had told him when the liner landed the *Grotkau's* men. He had preceesely hit oor time. I 'd hailed Bell for something to eat, an' he sent it o'er in the same boat wi' McRimmon, when the auld man came to me. He grinned an' slapped his legs an' worked his eyebrows the while I ate.

" 'How do Holdock, Steiner & Chase feed their men?' said he.

"'Ye can see,' I said, knockin' the top off another beer-bottle. 'I did not sign to be starved, McRimmon.'

"'Nor to swum, either,' said he, for Bell had tauld him how I carried the line aboard. 'Well, I'm thinkin' you'll be no loser. What freight could we ha' put into the *Lammergeyer* would equal salvage on four hunder thousand pounds — hull an' cargo? Eh, McPhee? This cuts the liver out o' Holdock, Steiner, Chase & Company, Limited. Eh, McPhee? An' I'm sufferin' from senile dementia now? Eh, McPhee? An' I'm not daft, am I, till I begin to paint the *Lammergeyer?* Eh, McPhee? Ye may weel lift your leg, Dandie! I ha' the laugh o' them all. Ye found watter in the engine-room?'

"'To speak wi'oot prejudice,' I said, 'there was some watter.'

"'They thought she was sinkin' after the propeller went. She filled wi' extraordinary rapeedity. Calder said it grieved him an' Bannister to abandon her.'

"I thought o' the dinner at Radley's, an' what like o' food I'd eaten for eight days.

"'It would grieve them sore,' I said.

"'But the crew would not hear o' stayin' an' workin' her back under canvas. They're gaun up an' down sayin' they'd ha' starved first.'

"'They'd ha' starved if they'd stayed,' said I.

" ' I tak' it, fra' Calder's account, there was a mutiny, a'most.'

" ' Ye know more than I, McRimmon,' I said. ' Speakin' wi'oot prejudice, for we're all in the same boat, *who* opened the bilge-cock ? '

" ' Oh, that's it — is it ? ' said the auld man, an' I could see he was surprised. ' A bilge-cock, ye say ? '

" ' I believe it was a bilge-cock. They were all shut when I came aboard, but some one had flooded the engine-room eight feet over all, an' shut it off with the worm-an'-wheel gear from the second gratin' afterwards.'

" ' Losh ! ' said McRimmon. ' The ineequity o' man's beyond belief. But it's awfu' discreditable to Holdock, Steiner & Chase, if that came oot in court.'

" ' It's just my own curiosity,' I said.

" ' Aweel, Dandie's afflicted wi' the same disease. Dandie, strive against curiosity, for it brings a little dog into traps an' such like. Whaur was the *Kite* when yon painted liner took off the *Grotkau's* people ? '

" ' Just there or thereabouts,' I said.

" ' An' which o' you twa thought to cover your lights ? ' said he, winkin'.

" ' Dandie,' I said to the dog, ' we must both strive against curiosity. It's an unremunerative business. What's our chance o' salvage, Dandie ? '

" He laughed till he choked. ' Tak' what I gie you, McPhee, an' be content,' he said. ' Lord, how a man wastes time when he gets old! Get aboard the *Kite*, mon, as soon as ye can. I've clean forgot there's a Baltic charter yammerin' for you at London. That'll be your last voyage, I'm thinkin', excep' by way o' pleasure.'

" Steiner's men were comin' aboard to take charge an' tow her round, an' I passed young Steiner in a boat as I went to the *Kite*. He looked down his nose; but McRimmon pipes up: 'Here's the man ye owe the *Grotkau* to — at a price, Steiner — at a price! Let me introduce Mr. McPhee to you. Maybe ye've met before; but ye've vara little luck in keepin' your men — ashore or afloat!'

" Young Steiner looked angry enough to eat him as he chuckled an' whustled in his dry old throat.

" ' Ye've not got your award yet,' Steiner says.

" ' Na, na,' says the auld man, in a screech ye could hear to the Hoe, ' but I've twa million sterlin', an' no bairns, ye Judeeas Apella, if ye mean to fight; an' I'll match ye p'und for p'und till the last p'und's oot. Ye ken *me*, Steiner! I'm McRimmon o' McNaughten & McRimmon!'

" ' Dod,' he said betwix' his teeth, sittin' back in the boat, ' I've waited fourteen year to break that Jew-firm, an' God be thankit I'll do it now.'

" The *Kite* was in the Baltic while the auld man
was warkin' his warks, but I know the assessors
valued the *Grotkau*, all told, at over three hunder
an' sixty thousand — her manifest was a treat o'
richness — an' McRimmon got a third for salvin'
an abandoned ship. Ye see, there's vast deeference
between towin' a ship wi' men on her an' pickin'
up a derelict — a vast deeference — in pounds
sterlin'. Moreover, twa three o' the *Grotkau's* crew
were burnin' to testify about food, an' there was a
note o' Calder to the Board, in regard to the tail-
shaft, that would ha' been vara damagin' if it had
come into court. They knew better than to fight.

" Syne the *Kite* came back, an' McRimmon
paid off me an' Bell personally, an' the rest of the
crew *pro rata*, I believe it's ca'ed. My share — oor
share, I should say — was just twenty-five thousand
pound sterlin'."

At this point Janet jumped up and kissed him.

" Five-an'-twenty thousand pound sterlin'. Noo,
I'm fra' the North, an' I'm not the like to fling
money awa' rashly, but I'd gie six months' pay —
one hunder an' twenty pounds — to know *who*
flooded the engine-room of the *Grotkau*. I'm fairly
well acquaint wi' McRimmon's eediosyncrasies, an'
he'd no hand in it. It was not Calder, for I've
asked him, an' he wanted to fight me. It would
be in the highest degree unprofessional o' Calder —
not fightin', but openin' bilge-cocks — but for a

while I thought it was him. Ay, I judged it might be him — under temptation."

" What's your theory? " I demanded.

" Weel, I'm inclined to think it was one o' those singular providences that remind us we're in the hands o' Higher Powers."

" It couldn't open and shut itself? "

" I did not mean that; but some half-starvin' oiler or, maybe, trimmer must ha' opened it a while to mak' sure o' leavin' the *Grotkau*. It's a demoralisin' thing to see an engine-room flood up after any accident to the gear — demoralisin' an' deceptive both. Aweel, the man got what he wanted, for they went aboard the liner cryin' that the *Grotkau* was sinkin'. But it's curious to think o' the consequences. In a' human probability, he's bein' damned in heaps at the present moment aboard another tramp freighter; an' here am I, wi' five-an'-twenty thousand pound invested, resolute to go to sea no more — providential's the preceese word — except as a passenger, ye'll understand, Janet."

* * * * * * * * * *

McPhee kept his word. He and Janet went for a voyage as passengers in the first-class saloon. They paid seventy pounds for their berths; and Janet found a very sick woman in the second-class saloon, so that for sixteen days she lived below, and chatted with the stewardesses at the foot of the second-saloon stairs while her patient slept. McPhee was a passenger for exactly twenty-four hours. Then the engineers' mess — where the oilcloth tables are — joyfully took him to its bosom, and for the rest of the voyage that company was richer by the unpaid services of a highly certificated engineer.

THE LANG MEN O' LARUT

THE LANG MEN O' LARUT [1]

THE Chief Engineer's sleeping-suit was of yellow striped with blue, and his speech was the speech of Aberdeen. They sluiced the deck under him, and he hopped on to the ornamental capstan, a black pipe between his teeth, though the hour was not seven of the morn.

" Did you ever hear o' the Lang Men o' Larut ? " he asked when the Man from Orizava had finished a story of an aboriginal giant discovered in the wilds of Brazil. There was never story yet passed the lips of teller, but the Man from Orizava could cap it.

" No, we never did," we responded with one voice. The Man from Orizava watched the Chief keenly, as a possible rival.

" I'm not telling the story for the sake of talking merely," said the Chief, " but as a warning against betting, unless you bet on a perrfect certainty. The Lang Men o' Larut were just a certainty. I have had talk wi' them. Now Larut, you will understand, is a dependency, or it may be an outlying

1 Copyright, 1891, by Macmillan & Co.

119

possession, o' the island o' Penang, and there they will get you tin and manganese, an' it may hap mica, and all manner o' meenerals. Larut is a great place."

"But what about the population?" said the Man from Orizava.

"The population," said the Chief, slowly, "were few but enorrmous. You must understand that, exceptin' the tin-mines, there is no special inducement to Europeans to reside in Larut. The climate is warm and remarkably like the climate o' Calcutta; and in regard to Calcutta, it cannot have escaped your obsairvation that — "

"Calcutta isn't Larut; and we've only just come from it," protested the Man from Orizava. "There's a meteorological department in Calcutta, too."

"Ay, but there's no meteorological department in Larut. Each man is a law to himself. Some drink whisky, and some drink *brandipanee*, and some drink cocktails — vara bad for the coats o' the stomach is a cocktail — and some drink sangaree, so I have been credibly informed; but one and all they sweat like the packing of a piston-head on a fourrteen-days' voyage with the screw racing half her time. But, as I was saying, the population o' Larut was five all told of English — that is to say, Scotch — an' I'm Scotch, ye know," said the Chief.

The Man from Orizava lit another cigarette, and waited patiently. It was hopeless to hurry the Chief Engineer.

"I am not pretending to account for the population o' Larut being laid down according to such fabulous dimensions. O' the five white men engaged upon the extraction o' tin ore and mercantile pursuits, there were three o' the sons o' Anak. Wait while I remember. Lammitter was the first by two inches — a giant in the land, an' a terreefic man to cross in his ways. From heel to head he was six feet nine inches, and proportionately built across and through the thickness of his body. Six good feet nine inches — an overbearin' man. Next to him, and I have forgotten his precise business, was Sandy Vowle. And he was six feet seven, but lean and lathy, and it was more in the elasteecity of his neck that the height lay than in any honesty o' bone and sinew. Five feet and a few odd inches may have been his real height. The remainder came out when he held up his head, and six feet seven he was upon the door-sills. I took his measure in chalk standin' on a chair. And next to him, but a proportionately made man, ruddy and of a fair countenance, was Jock Coan — that they called the Fir Cone. He was but six feet five, and a child beside Lammitter and Vowle. When the three walked out together, they made a scunner run through the colony o'

Larut. The Malays ran round them as though
they had been the giant trees in the Yosemite
Valley — these three Lang Men o' Larut. It was
perfectly ridiculous — a *lusus naturæ* — that one
little place should have contained maybe the three
tallest ordinar' men upon the face o' the earth.

"Obsairve now the order o' things. For it led
to the finest big drink in Larut, and six sore heads
the morn that endured for a week. I am against
immoderate liquor, but the event to follow was a
justification. You must understand that many
coasting steamers call at Larut wi' strangers o' the
mercantile profession. In the springtime, when
the young cocoanuts were ripening, and the trees
o' the forests were putting forth their leaves, there
came an American man to Larut, and he was six
foot three, or it may have been four, in his stockings. He came on business from Sacramento, but
he stayed for pleasure wi' the Lang Men o' Larut.
Less than a half o' the population were ordinar' in
their girth and stature, ye will understand — How-
son and Nailor, merchants, five feet nine or thereabouts. He had business with those two, and he
stood above them from the six feet threedom o'
his height till they went to drink. In the course
o' conversation he said, as tall men will, things
about his height, and the trouble of it to him.
That was his pride o' the flesh.

" 'As the longest man in the island — ' he

said, but there they took him up and asked if he were sure.

"'I say I am the longest man in the island,' he said, 'and on that I'll bet my substance.'

"They laid down the bed-plates of a big drink then and there, and put it aside while they called Jock Coan from his house, near by among the fireflies' winking.

"'How's a' wi' you?' said Jock, and came in by the side o' the Sacramento profligate, two inches, or it may have been one, taller than he.

"'You're long,' said the man, opening his eyes. 'But I am longer.' An' they sent a whistle through the night an' howkit out Sandy Vowle from his bit bungalow, and he came in an' stood by the side o' Jock, an' the pair just fillit the room to the ceiling-cloth.

"The Sacramento man was a euchre-player and a most profane sweerer. 'You hold both Bowers,' he said, 'but the Joker is with me.'

"'Fair an' softly,' says Nailor. 'Jock, whaur's Lang Lammitter?'

"'Here,' says that man, putting his leg through the window and coming in like an anaconda o' the desert furlong by furlong, one foot in Penang and one in Batavia, and a hand in North Borneo it may be.

"'Are you suited?' said Nailor, when the hinder end o' Lang Lammitter was slidden through the sill an' the head of Lammitter was lost in the smoke away above.

"The American man took out his card and put it on the table. 'Esdras B. Longer is my name, America is my nation, 'Frisco is my resting-place, but this here beats Creation,' said he. 'Boys, giants — side-show giants — I minded to slide out of my bet if I had been overtopped, on the strength of the riddle on this pasteboard. I would have done it if you had topped me even by three inches, but when it comes to feet — yards — miles, I am not the man to shirk the biggest drink that ever made the travellers'-joy palm blush with virginal indignation, or the orang-outang and the peram-bulating dyak howl with envy. Set them up and continue till the final conclusion.'

"O mon, I tell you 'twas an awful sight to see those four giants threshing about the house and the island, and tearin' down the pillars thereof an' throwing palm-trees broadcast, and currling their long legs round the hills o' Larut. An awfu' sight! I was there. I did not mean to tell you, but it's out now. I was not overcome, for I e'en sat me down under the pieces o' the table at four the morn an' meditated upon the strangeness of things.

"Losh, yon's the breakfast-bell!"

"BRUGGLESMITH"

"BRUGGLESMITH" [1]

This day the ship went down, and all hands was drowned
but me.—*Clark Russell.*

THE first officer of the *Breslau* asked me to dinner
on board, before the ship went round to Southampton to pick up her passengers. The *Breslau*
was lying below London Bridge, her fore-hatches
opened for cargo, and her deck littered with nuts
and bolts, and screws and chains. The Black
McPhee had been putting some finishing touches
to his adored engines, and McPhee is the most
tidy of chief engineers. If the leg of a cock-
roach gets into one of his slide-valves the whole
ship knows it, and half the ship has to clean up
the mess.

After dinner, which the first officer, McPhee,
and I ate in one little corner of the empty saloon,
McPhee returned to the engine-room to attend to
some brass-fitters. The first officer and I smoked
on the bridge and watched the lights of the
crowded shipping till it was time for me to go

1 Copyright, 1893, by D. Appleton & Co.

home. It seemed, in the pauses of our conversation, that I could catch an echo of fearful bellowings from the engine-room, and the voice of McPhee singing of home and the domestic affections.

"McPhee has a friend aboard to-night—a man who was a boiler-maker at Greenock when McPhee was a 'prentice," said the first officer. "I didn't ask him to dine with us because — "

"I see — I mean I hear," I answered. We talked on for a few minutes longer, and McPhee came up from the engine-room with his friend on his arm.

"Let me present ye to this gentleman," said McPhee. "He's a great admirer o' your wor-rks. He has just hear-rd o' them."

McPhee could never pay a compliment prettily. The friend sat down suddenly on a bollard, saying that McPhee had understated the truth. Personally, he on the bollard considered that Shakespeare was trembling in the balance solely on my account, and if the first officer wished to dispute this he was prepared to fight the first officer then or later, "as per invoice." "Man, if ye only knew," said he, wagging his head, "the times I've lain in my lonely bunk reading 'Vanity Fair' an' sobbin'— ay, weepin' bitterly, at the pure fascination of it."

He shed a few tears for guarantee of good faith, and the first officer laughed. McPhee resettled the man's hat, that had tilted over one eyebrow, and said:

"That'll wear off in a little. It's just the smell o' the engine-room," said McPhee.

"I think I'll wear off myself," I whispered to the first officer. "Is the dinghy ready?"

The dinghy was at the gangway, which was down, and the first officer went forward to find a man to row me to the bank. He returned with a very sleepy Lascar, who knew the river.

"Are you going?" said the man on the bollard. "Well, I'll just see ye home. McPhee, help me down the gangway. It has as many ends as a cat-o'-nine tails, and — losh! — how innumerable are the dinghys!"

"You'd better let him come with you," said the first officer. "Muhammad Jan, put the drunk sahib ashore first. Take the sober sahib to the next stairs."

I had my foot in the bow of the dinghy, the tide was making up-stream, when the man cannoned against me, pushed the Lascar back on the gang-way, cast loose the painter, and the dinghy began to saw, stern-first, along the side of the *Breslau*.

"We'll have no exter-r-raneous races here," said the man. "I've known the Thames for thirty years — "

There was no time for argument. We were drifting under the *Breslau's* stern, and I knew

129

that her propeller was half out of water, in the midst of an inky tangle of buoys, low-lying hawsers, and moored ships, with the tide roaring about them.

" What shall I do ? " I shouted to the first officer.

" Find the Police Boat as soon as you can, and for God's sake get way on the dinghy. Steer with the oar. The rudder's unshipped and — "

I could hear no more. The dinghy slid away, bumped on a mooring-buoy, swung round and jigged off irresponsibly as I hunted for the oar. The man sat in the bow, his chin on his hands, smiling.

" Row, you ruffian," I said. " Get her out into the middle of the river — "

" It's a preevilege to gaze on the face o' genius. Let me go on thinking. There was 'Little Barnaby Dorrit' and 'The Mystery o' the Bleak Druid.' I sailed in a ship called the *Druid* once — badly found she was. It all comes back to me so sweet. It all comes back to me. Man, ye steer like a genius ! "

We just bumped another mooring-buoy and drifted on to the bows of a Norwegian timbership — I could see the great square holes on either side of the cut-water. Then we dived into a string of barges and scraped through them by the paint on our planks. It was a consolation to think that

the dinghy was being reduced in value at every
bump, but the question before me was when she
would begin to leak. The man looked ahead into
the pitchy darkness and whistled.

" Yon's a Castle liner; her ties are black. She's
swinging across stream. Keep her port light on
our starboard bow, and go large," he said.

"How can I keep anything anywhere? You're
sitting on the oars. Row, man, if you don't want
to drown."

He took the sculls, saying sweetly: " No harm
comes to a drunken man. That's why I wish to
come with *you*. Man, ye're not fit to be alone in
a boat."

He flirted the dinghy round the big ship, and
for the next ten minutes I enjoyed — positively
enjoyed — an exhibition of first-class steering.
We threaded in and out of the mercantile marine
of Great Britain as a ferret threads a rabbit-hole,
and we, he that is to say, sang joyously to each
ship till men looked over bulwarks and cursed us.
When we came to some moderately clear water
he gave the sculls to me, and said :

" If ye could row as ye write, I'd respect you
for all your vices. Yon's London Bridge. Take
her through."

We shot under the dark ringing arch, and came
out the other side, going up swiftly with the tide
chanting songs of victory. Except that I wished

to get home before morning, I was growing reconciled to the jaunt. There were one or two stars visible, and by keeping into the centre of the stream, I could not come to any very serious danger.

The man began to sing loudly:

> " The smartest clipper that you could find,
>   Yo ho !   Oho !
>   Was the *Marg'ret Evans* of the Black X Line
>   A hundred years ago !

Incorporate that in your next book. Which is marvellous." Here he stood up in the bows and declaimed :

> " Ye Towers o' Julia, London's lasting wrong,
>   By mony a foul an' midnight murder fed —
>   Sweet Thames run softly till I end my song —
>   And yon's the grave as little as my bed.

I'm a poet mysel' an' I can feel for others."

"Sit down," said I. "You'll have the boat over."

" Ay, I'm settin' — settin' like a hen." He plumped down heavily, and added, shaking his forefinger at me :

> " Lear-rn, prudent, cautious self-control
>   Is wisdom's root.

How did a man o' your parts come to be so drunk? Oh, it's a sinfu' thing, an' ye may thank God on all fours that I'm wi' you.   What's yon boat ? "

We had drifted far up the river, and a boat manned by four men, who rowed with a soothingly regular stroke, was overhauling us.

" It's the River Police," I said, at the top of my voice.

" Oh ay ! If your sin do not find you out on dry land, it will find you out in the deep waters. Is it like they'll give us drink ? "

" Exceedingly likely. I'll hail them." I hailed.

" What are you doing ? " was the answer from the boat.

" It's the *Breslau's* dinghy broken loose," I began.

" It's a vara drunken man broke loose," roared my companion, " and I'm taking him home by water, for he cannot stand on dry land." Here he shouted my name twenty times running, and I could feel the blushes racing over my body three deep.

" You'll be locked up in ten minutes, my friend," I said, " and I don't think you'll be bailed either."

" H'sh, man, h'sh. They think I'm your uncle." He caught up a scull and began splashing the boat as it ranged alongside.

" You're a nice pair," said the sergeant at last.

" I am anything you please so long as you take this fiend away. Tow us in to the nearest station, and I'll make it worth your while," I said.

" Corruption — corruption," roared the man,

throwing himself flat in the bottom of the boat.
"Like unto the worms that perish, so is man. And
all for the sake of a filthy half-crown to be arrested
by the River Police at my time o' life!"

"For pity's sake, row," I shouted. "The man's
drunk."

They rowed us to a flat — a fire- or a police-
station; it was too dark to see which. I could
feel that they regarded me in no better light than
my companion, and I could not explain, for I was
holding the far end of the painter, ten long feet
from all respectability.

We got out of the boat, my companion falling
flat on his wicked face, and the sergeant asked us
rude questions about the dinghy. My companion
washed his hands of all responsibility. He was
an old man; he had been lured into a stolen boat
by a young man — probably a thief — he had
saved the boat from wreck (this was absolutely
true), and now he expected salvage in the shape
of hot whisky and water. The sergeant turned
to me. Fortunately I was in evening dress, and
had a card to show. More fortunately still, the
sergeant happened to know the *Breslau* and
McPhee. He promised to send the dinghy down
next tide, and was not beyond accepting my
thanks, in silver.

As this was satisfactorily arranged, I heard my
companion say angrily to a constable, "If you

will not give it to a dry man, ye maun to a drookit." Then he walked deliberately off the edge of the flat into the water. Somebody stuck a boat-hook into his clothes and hauled him out.

"Now," said he, triumphantly, "under the rules o' the R-royal Humane Society, ye must give me hot whisky and water. Do not put temptation before the laddie. He's my nephew an' a good boy i' the main. Tho' why he should masquerade as Mister Thackeray on the high seas is beyond my comprehension. Oh, the vanity o' youth! McPhee told me ye were as vain as a peacock. I mind that now."

"You had better give him something to drink and wrap him up for the night. I don't know who he is," I said desperately; and when the man had settled down to a drink supplied on my representations, I escaped and found that I was near a bridge.

I went towards Fleet Street, intending to take a hansom and go home. After the first feeling of indignation died out, the absurdity of the experience struck me fully, and I began to laugh aloud in the empty streets, to the scandal of a policeman. The more I reflected the more heartily I laughed, till my mirth was quenched by a hand on my shoulder, and turning I saw him who should have been in bed at the river police-station. He was damp all over; his wet silk hat rode far at the back of his head, and round his shoulders hung a striped yellow blanket, evidently the property of the State.

"The crackling o' thorns under a pot," said he, solemnly. "Laddie, have ye not thought o' the sin of idle laughter? My heart misgave me that ever ye'd get home, an' I've just come to convoy you a piece. They're sore uneducate down there by the river. They wouldna listen to me when I talked o' your wor-rks, so I e'en left them. Cast the blanket about you, laddie. It's fine and cold."

I groaned inwardly. Providence evidently intended that I should frolic through eternity with McPhee's infamous acquaintance.

"Go away," I said; "go home, or I'll give you in charge."

He leaned against a lamp-post and laid his finger to his nose—his dishonourable, carnelian neb.

"I mind now that McPhee told me ye were vainer than a peacock, an' your castin' me adrift in a boat shows ye were drunker than an owl. A good name is as a savoury bakemeat. I ha' nane." He smacked his lips joyously.

"Well, I know that," I said.

"Ay, but *ye* have. I mind now that McPhee spoke o' your reputation that you're so proud of. Laddie, if ye gie me in charge — I'm old enough to be your father — I'll bla-ast your reputation as far as my voice can carry; for I'll call you by

name till the cows come hame. It's no jestin'
matter to be a friend to me. If you discard my
friendship, ye must come to Vine Street wi' me
for stealin' the *Breslau's* dinghy."

Then he sang at the top of his voice:

> "In the mor-rnin',
> I' the mor-rnin' by the black van —
> We'll toodle up to Vine Street i' the mornin'!

Yon's my own composeetion, but *I'm* not vain.
We'll go home together, laddie, we'll go home together." And he sang "Auld Lang Syne" to show
that he meant it.

A policeman suggested that we had better move
on, and we moved on to the Law Courts near St.
Clement Danes. My companion was quieter now,
and his speech, which up till that time had been
distinct — it was a marvel to see how in his condition he could talk dialect — began to slur and
slide and slummock. He bade me observe the
architecture of the Law Courts and linked himself lovingly to my arm. Then he saw a policeman, and before I could shake him off, whirled
me up to the man singing:

> "Every member of the Force
> Has a watch and chain of course —"

and threw his dripping blanket over the helmet
of the Law. In any other country in the world

we should have run an exceedingly good chance
of being shot, or dirked, or clubbed — and club-
bing is worse than being shot. But I reflected in
that wet-cloth tangle that this was England, where
the police are made to be banged and battered and
bruised, that they may the better endure a police-
court reprimand next morning. We three fell in
a tangle, he calling on me by name — that was
the tingling horror of it — to sit on the policeman's head and cut the traces. I wriggled clear
first and shouted to the policeman to kill the
blanket-man.

Naturally the policeman answered : " You're as
bad as 'im," and chased me, as the smaller man,
round St. Clement Danes into Holywell Street,
where I ran into the arms of another policeman.
That flight could not have lasted more than a
minute and a half, but it seemed to me as long
and as wearisome as the foot-bound flight of a
nightmare. I had leisure to think of a thousand
things as I ran, but most I thought of the great
and godlike man who held a sitting in the north
gallery of St. Clement Danes a hundred years ago.
I know that he at least would have felt for me.
So occupied was I with these considerations, that
when the other policeman hugged me to his bosom
and said : " What are you tryin' to do ? " I answered with exquisite politeness : " Sir, let us take
a walk down Fleet Street." " Bow Street 'll do

your business, I think," was the answer, and for a moment I thought so too, till it seemed I might wriggle out of it. Then there was a hideous scene, and it was complicated by my companion hurrying up with the blanket and telling me — always by name — that he would rescue me or perish in the attempt.

" Knock him down," I pleaded. " Club his head open first and I'll explain afterwards."

The first policeman, the one who had been outraged, drew his truncheon and cut my companion's head. The high silk hat crackled and the owner dropped like a log.

" Now you've done it," I said. " You've probably killed him."

Holywell Street never goes to bed. A small crowd gathered on the spot, and some one of German extraction cried: " You haf killed the man."

Another cried: " Take his bloomin' number. I saw him strook cruel 'ard. Yah ! "

Now, the street was empty when the trouble began, and, saving the two policemen and myself, no one had seen the blow. I said, therefore, in a loud and cheerful voice :

" The man's a friend of mine. He's fallen down in a fit. Bobby, will you bring the ambulance ? " Under my breath I added : " It's five shillings apiece, and the man didn't hit you."

"No, but 'im and you tried to scrob me," said the policeman.

This was not a thing to argue about.

"Is Dempsey on duty at Charing Cross?" I said.

"Wot d' you know of Dempsey, you bloomin' garrotter?" said the policeman.

"If Dempsey's there, he knows me. Get the ambulance quick, and I'll take him to Charing Cross."

"You're coming to Bow Street, *you* are," said the policeman, crisply.

"The man's dying"— he lay groaning on the pavement — "get the ambulance," said I.

There is an ambulance at the back of St. Clement Danes, whereof I know more than most people. The policeman seemed to possess the keys of the box in which it lived. We trundled it out — it was a three-wheeled affair with a hood — and we bundled the body of the man upon it.

A body in an ambulance looks very extremely dead. The policemen softened at the sight of the stiff boot-heels.

"Now, then," said they, and I fancied that they still meant Bow Street.

"Let me see Dempsey for three minutes if he's on duty," I answered.

"Very good. He is."

Then I knew that all would be well, but before

we started I put my head under the ambulance-hood to see if the man were alive. A guarded whisper caught my ear.

"Laddie, you maun pay me for a new hat. They've broken it. Dinna desert me now, laddie. I'm o'er old to go to Bow Street in my grey hairs for a fault of yours. Laddie, dinna desert me."

"You'll be lucky if you get off under seven years," I said to the policeman.

Moved by a very lively fear of having exceeded their duty, the two policemen left their beats, and the mournful procession wound down the empty Strand. Once west of the Adelphi, I knew I should be in my own country; and the policemen had reason to know that too, for as I was pacing proudly a little ahead of the catafalque, another policeman said "Good night, sir," to me as he passed.

"Now, you see," I said, with condescension, "I wouldn't be in your shoes for something. On my word, I've a great mind to march you two down to Scotland Yard."

"If the gentleman's a friend o' yours, per'aps—" said the policeman who had given the blow, and was reflecting on the consequences.

"Perhaps you'd like me to go away and say nothing about it," I said. Then there hove into view the figure of Constable Dempsey, glittering in his oilskins, and an angel of light to me. I had known him for months; he was an esteemed friend of mine, and we used to talk together in the early mornings. The fool seeks to ingratiate himself with Princes and Ministers; and courts and cabinets leave him to perish miserably. The wise man makes allies among the police and the hansoms, so that his friends spring up from the roundhouse and the cab-rank, and even his offences become triumphal processions.

"Dempsey," said I, "have the Police been on strike again? They've put some things on duty at St. Clement Danes that want to take me to Bow Street for garrotting."

"Lor', sir!" said Dempsey, indignantly.

"Tell them I'm not a garrotter, nor a thief. It's simply disgraceful that a gentleman can't walk down the Strand without being man-handled by these roughs. One of them has done his best to kill my friend here; and I'm taking the body home. Speak for me, Dempsey."

There was no time for the much-misrepresented policemen to say a word. Dempsey spoke to them in language calculated to alarm. They tried to explain, but Dempsey launched into a glowing catalogue of my virtues, as noted by him in the early hours. "And," he concluded vehemently, "'e writes for the papers, too. How'd *you* like to be written for in the papers — in verse, too, which is 'is 'abit. You leave 'im alone. 'Im an' me have been friends for months."

"What about the dead man?" said the policeman who had not given the blow.

"I'll tell you," I said, relenting, and to the three policemen under the lights of Charing Cross assembled, I recounted faithfully and at length the adventures of the night, beginning with the *Breslau* and ending at St. Clement Danes. I described the sinful old ruffian in the ambulance in terms that made him wriggle where he lay, and never since the Metropolitan Police was founded did three policemen laugh as those three laughed. The Strand echoed to it, and the unclean birds of the night stood and wondered.

"Oh, lor'!" said Dempsey, wiping his eyes, "I'd ha' given anything to see that old man runnin' about with a wet blanket an' all! Excuse me, sir, but you ought to get took up every night for to make us 'appy." He dissolved into fresh guffaws.

There was a clinking of silver, and the two policemen of St. Clement Danes hurried back to their beats, laughing as they ran.

"Take 'im to Charing Cross," said Dempsey between shouts. "They'll send the ambulance back in the morning."

"Laddie, ye've misca'ed me shameful names, but I'm o'er old to go to a hospital. Dinna desert me, laddie; tak' me home to my wife," said the voice in the ambulance.

"He's none so bad. 'Is wife'll comb 'is hair for 'im proper," said Dempsey, who was a married man.

"Where d' you live?" I demanded.

"Brugglesmith," was the answer.

"What's that?" I said to Dempsey, more skilled than I in the portmanteau words of early dawn.

"Brook Green, 'Ammersmith," Dempsey translated promptly.

"Of course," I said. "That's just the sort of place he would choose to live in. I only wonder it was not Kew."

"Are you going to wheel 'im 'ome, sir?" said Dempsey.

"I'd wheel him home if he lived in — Paradise. He's not going to get out of this ambulance while I'm here. He'd drag me into a murder for tuppence."

"Then strap 'im up an' make sure," said Dempsey, and he deftly buckled two straps, that hung by the side of the ambulance, over the man's body. Brugglesmith — I know not his other name — was sleeping deeply. He even smiled in his sleep.

"That's all right," said Dempsey, and I moved off, wheeling my devil's perambulator before me. Trafalgar Square was empty except for the few that slept in the open. One of these wretches ranged alongside and begged for money, asserting that he had once been a gentleman.

"So have I," I said. "That was long ago. I'll give you a shilling if you'll help me to push this thing."

"Is it a murder?" said the vagabond, shrinking back. "I've not got to *that* yet."

"No. It's going to be one," I answered. "I have."

The man slunk back into the darkness, and I pressed on, through Cockspur Street, and up to Piccadilly Circus, wondering what I should do with my treasure. All London was asleep, and I had only this drunken carcass to bear me company. It was silent — silent as chaste Piccadilly. A young man of my acquaintance came out of a pink-brick club as I passed. A faded carnation drooped from his buttonhole; he had been playing cards, and was walking home before the dawn, when he overtook me.

"What are you doing?" he said.

I was far beyond any feeling of shame. "It's for a bet," said I. "Come and help."

"Laddie, who's yon?" said the voice beneath the hood.

"Good Lord!" said the young man, leaping across the pavement. Perhaps card-losses had told on his nerves. Mine were steel that night.

"The Lord, the Lord?" the passionless, incurious voice went on. "Dinna be profane, laddie. He'll come in His ain good time."

The young man looked at me with horror.

"It's all part of the bet," I answered. "Do come and push."

"W — where are you going to?" said he.

"Brugglesmith," said the voice within. "Laddie, d' ye ken my wife?"

"No," said I.

"Well, she's just a tremenjus wumman. Laddie, I want a drink. Knock at one o' these braw houses, laddie, an' — an' — ye may kiss the girl for your pains."

"Lie still, or I'll gag you," I said savagely.

The young man with the carnation crossed to the other side of Piccadilly, and hailed the only hansom visible for miles. What he thought I cannot tell. Later I was told.

I pressed on — wheeling, eternally wheeling — to Brook Green, Hammersmith. There I would abandon Brugglesmith to the gods of that desolate land. We had been through so much together that I could not leave him bound in the street. Besides, he would call after me, and oh! it is a shameful thing to hear one's name ringing down the emptiness of London in the dawn.

So I went on, past Apsley House, even to the coffee-stall, but there was no coffee for Brugglesmith. And into Knightsbridge — respectable Knightsbridge — I wheeled my burden, the body of Brugglesmith.

146

" Laddie, what are ye going to do to me ? " he said, when opposite the barracks.

" Kill you," I said briefly, " or hand you over to your wife. Be quiet."

He would not obey. He talked incessantly — sliding in one sentence from clear-cut dialect to wild and drunken jumble. At the Albert Hall he said that I was the " Hattle Gardle buggle," which I apprehend is the Hatton Garden burglar. At Kensington High Street he loved me as a son, but when my weary legs came to the Addison Road Bridge he implored me with tears to unloose the straps and to fight against the sin of vanity. No man molested us. It was as though a bar had been set between myself and all humanity till I had cleared my account with Bruggiesmith. The glimmering of light grew in the sky ; the cloudy brown of the wood pavement turned to heather-purple ; I made no doubt that I should be allowed vengeance on Brugglesmith ere the evening.

At Hammersmith the heavens were steel-grey, and the day came weeping. All the tides of the sadness of an unprofitable dawning poured into the soul of Brugglesmith. He wept bitterly, because the puddles looked cold and houseless. I entered a half-waked public-house — in evening dress and an ulster, I marched to the bar — and got him whisky on condition that he should cease kicking at the canvas of the ambulance. Then

he wept more bitterly, for that he had ever been
associated with me, and so seduced into stealing
the *Breslau's* dinghy.

The day was white and wan when I reached
my long journey's end, and, putting back the
hood, bade Brugglesmith declare where he lived.
His eyes wandered disconsolately round the red-
and- grey houses till they fell on a villa in whose
garden stood a staggering board with the legend
" To Let." It needed only this to break him
down utterly, and with that breakage fled his fine
fluency in his guttural northern tongue; for liquor
levels all.

"Olely lil while," he sobbed. "Olely lil while.
Home — falmy — besht of falmies — wife, too —
you dole know my wife! Left them all a lil while
ago. Now everything's sold—all sold. Wife —
falmy — all sold. Lemmegellup!"

I unbuckled the straps cautiously. Brugglesmith rolled off his resting-place and staggered
to the house.

" Wattle I do?" he said.

Then I understood the baser depths in the
mind of Mephistopheles.

" Ring," I said; "perhaps they are in the attic
or the cellar."

" You do' know my wife. She shleeps on soful
in the dorlin'-room waitin' meculhome. *You* do'
know my wife."

He took off his boots, covered them with his tall hat, and craftily as a Red Indian picked his way up the garden path and smote the bell marked "Visitors" a severe blow with his clinched fist.

"Bell sole too. Sole electick bell! Wassor bell this? I can't riggle bell," he moaned despairingly.

"You pull it — pull it hard," I repeated, keeping a wary eye down the road. Vengeance was coming, and I desired no witnesses.

"Yes, I'll pull it hard." He slapped his forehead with inspiration. "I'll pull it out."

Leaning back, he grasped the knob with both hands and pulled. A wild ringing in the kitchen was his answer. Spitting on his hands, he pulled with renewed strength, and shouted for his wife. Then he bent his ear to the knob, shook his head, drew out an enormous yellow-and-red handkerchief, tied it round the knob, turned his back to the door, and pulled over his shoulder.

Either the handkerchief or the wire, it seemed to me, was bound to give way. But I had forgotten the bell. Something cracked in the kitchen, and Brugglesmith moved slowly down the doorsteps, pulling valiantly. Three feet of wire followed him.

"Pull, oh, pull!" I cried. "It's coming now!"
"Qui' ri'," he said. "*I'll* riggle bell."

He bowed forward, the wire creaking and straining behind him, the bell-knob clasped to his bosom, and from the noises within I fancied the bell was taking away with it half the woodwork of the kitchen and all the basement banisters as it came up.

"Get a purchase on her," I shouted, and he spun round, lapping that good copper wire about him. I opened the garden gate politely, and he passed out, spinning his own cocoon. Still the bell came up, hand over hand, and still the wire held fast. He was in the middle of the road now, whirling like an impaled cockchafer, and shouting madly for his wife and family. There he met with the ambulance, the bell within the house gave one last peal, and bounded from the far end of the hall to the inner side of the hall door, when it stayed fast. So did not my friend Brugglesmith. He fell upon his face, embracing the ambulance as he did so, and the two turned over together in the toils of the never-sufficiently-to-be-advertised copper wire.

"Laddie," he gasped, his speech returning, "have I a legal remedy?"

"I will go and look for one," I said, and, departing, found two policemen, whom I told that daylight had surprised a burglar in Brook Green while he was stealing lead from an empty house. Perhaps they had better take care of that bootless thief. He seemed to be in difficulties.

I led the way to the spot, and behold! in the splendour of the dawning, the ambulance, wheels uppermost, was walking down the muddy road on two stockinged feet — was shuffling to and fro in a quarter of a circle whose radius was copper wire, and whose centre was the bell-plate of the empty house.

Next to the amazing ingenuity with which Brugglesmith had contrived to lash himself under the ambulance, the thing that appeared to impress the constables most was the fact of the St. Clement Danes ambulance being at Brook Green, Hammersmith.

They even asked me, of all the people in the world, whether I knew anything about it.

*   *   *   *   *   *   *   *   *   *

They extricated him; not without pain and dirt. He explained that he was repelling boarding-attacks by a " Hattle Gardle buggle " who had sold his house, wife, and family. As to the bell-wire, he offered no explanation, and was borne off shoulder-high between the two policemen. Though his feet were not within six inches of the ground, they paddled swiftly, and I saw that in his magnificent mind he was running — furiously running.

Sometimes I have wondered whether he wished to find me.

AN ERROR IN
THE FOURTH DIMENSION

AN ERROR IN
THE FOURTH DIMENSION

BEFORE he was thirty, he discovered that there was
no one to play with him. Though the wealth of
three toilsome generations stood to his account,
though his tastes in the matter of books, bindings,
rugs, swords, bronzes, lacquer, pictures, plate, stat-
uary, horses, conservatories, and agriculture were
educated and catholic, the public opinion of his
country wanted to know why he did not go to
office daily, as his father had before him.

So he fled, and they howled behind him that he
was an unpatriotic Anglomaniac, born to consume
fruits, one totally lacking in public spirit. He
wore an eye-glass; he had built a wall round his
country house, with a high gate that shut, instead
of inviting America to sit on his flower-beds; he
ordered his clothes from England; and the press
of his abiding city cursed him, from his eye-glass
to his trousers, for two consecutive days.

When he rose to light again, it was where nothing less than the tents of an invading army in
Piccadilly would make any difference to anybody.

If he had money and leisure, England stood ready to give him all that money and leisure could buy. That price paid, she would ask no questions. He took his cheque-book and accumulated things — warily at first, for he remembered that in America things own the man. To his delight, he discovered that in England he could put his belongings under his feet; for classes, ranks, and denominations of people rose, as it were, from the earth, and silently and discreetly took charge of his possessions. They had been born and bred for that sole purpose — servants of the cheque-book. When that was at an end they would depart as mysteriously as they had come.

The impenetrability of this regulated life irritated him, and he strove to learn something of the human side of these people. He retired baffled, to be trained by his menials. In America, the native demoralises the English servant. In England, the servant educates the master. Wilton Sargent strove to learn all they taught as ardently as his father had striven to wreck, before capture, the railways of his native land; and it must have been some touch of the old bandit railway blood that bade him buy, for a song, Holt Hangars, whose forty-acre lawn, as every one knows, sweeps down in velvet to the quadruple tracks of the Great Buchonian Railway. Their trains flew by almost continuously, with a bee-like drone in the

day and a flutter of strong wings at night. The
son of Merton Sargent had good right to be interested in them. He owned controlling interests in
several thousand miles of track — not permanent
way — built on altogether different plans, where
locomotives eternally whistled for grade-crossings,
and parlour-cars of fabulous expense and unrestful
design skated round curves that the Great Buchonian would have condemned as unsafe in a con-
struction line. From the edge of his lawn he could
trace the chaired metals falling away, rigid as a
bowstring, into the valley of the Prest, studded
with the long perspective of the block signals,
buttressed with stone, and carried, high above all
possible risk, on a forty-foot embankment.

Left to himself, he would have builded a private
car, and kept it at the nearest railway-station, Amberley Royal, five miles away. But those into
whose hands he had committed himself for his
English training had little knowledge of railways
and less of private cars. The one they knew was
something that existed in the scheme of things for
their convenience. The other they held to be
"distinctly American"; and, with the versatility
of his race, Wilton Sargent had set out to be just
a little more English than the English.

He succeeded to admiration. He learned not
to redecorate Holt Hangars, though he warmed
it; to leave his guests alone; to refrain from su-

perfluous introductions; to abandon manners of
which he had great store, and to hold fast by
manner which can after labour be acquired. He
learned to let other people, hired for the purpose,
attend to the duties for which they were paid. He
learned — this he got from a ditcher on the estate
— that every man with whom he came in contact
had his decreed position in the fabric of the realm,
which position he would do well to consult. Last
mystery of all, he learned to golf — well: and
when an American knows the innermost mean-
ing of "Don't press, slow back, and keep your
eye on the ball," he is, for practical purposes,
denationalised.

His other education proceeded on the pleasant-
est lines. Was he interested in any conceivable
thing in heaven above, or the earth beneath, or
the waters under the earth? Forthwith appeared
at his table, guided by those safe hands into which
he had fallen, the very men who had best said,
done, written, explored, excavated, built, launched,
created, or studied that one thing — herders of
books and prints in the British Museum; special-
ists in scarabs, cartouches, and dynasties Egyptian;
rovers and raiders from the heart of unknown
lands; toxicologists; orchid-hunters; monogra-
phers on flint implements, carpets, prehistoric
man, or early Renaissance music. They came,
and they played with him. They asked no ques-

tions; they cared not so much as a pin who or
what he was. They demanded only that he
should be able to talk and listen courteously.
Their work was done elsewhere and out of his
sight.

There were also women.

"Never," said Wilton Sargent to himself, "has
an American seen England as I'm seeing it"; and
he thought, blushing beneath the bedclothes, of
the unregenerate and blatant days when he would
steam to office, down the Hudson, in his twelve-
hundred-ton ocean-going steam-yacht, and arrive,
by gradations, at Bleecker Street, hanging on to a
leather strap between an Irish washerwoman and
a German anarchist. If any of his guests had
seen him then they would have said: "How distinctly American!" and — Wilton did not care
for that tone. He had schooled himself to an
English walk, and, so long as he did not raise it,
an English voice. He did not gesticulate with
his hands; he sat down on most of his enthusiasms,
but he could not rid himself of The Shibboleth.
He would ask for the Worcestershire sauce: even
Howard, his immaculate butler, could not break
him of this.

It was decreed that he should complete his education in a wild and wonderful manner, and, further,
that I should be in at that death.

Wilton had more than once asked me to Holt

Hangars, for the purpose of showing how well the new life fitted him, and each time I had declared it creaseless. His third invitation was more informal than the others, and he hinted of some matter in which he was anxious for my sympathy or counsel, or both. There is room for an infinity of mistakes when a man begins to take liberties with his nationality; and I went down expecting things. A seven-foot dog-cart and a groom in the black Holt Hangars livery met me at Amberley Royal. At Holt Hangars I was received by a person of elegance and true reserve, and piloted to my luxurious chamber. There were no other guests in the house, and this set me thinking.

Wilton came into my room about half an hour before dinner, and though his face was masked with a drop-curtain of highly embroidered indifference, I could see that he was not at ease. In time, for he was then almost as difficult to move as one of my own countrymen, I extracted the tale — simple in its extravagance, extravagant in its simplicity. It seemed that Hackman of the British Museum had been staying with him about ten days before, boasting of scarabs. Hackman has a way of carrying really priceless antiquities on his tie-ring and in his trouser pockets. Apparently, he had intercepted something on its way to the Boulak Museum which, he said, was "a genuine Amen-Hotep — a queen's scarab of the Fourth

Dynasty." Now Wilton had bought from Cassavetti, whose reputation is not above suspicion, a
scarab of much the same scarabeousness, and had
left it in his London chambers. Hackman at a
venture, but knowing Cassavetti, pronounced it an
imposition. There was long discussion — savant
versus millionaire, one saying: "But I know it
cannot be"; and the other: "But I can and will
prove it." Wilton found it necessary for his soul's
satisfaction to go up to town, then and there — a
forty-mile run — and bring back the scarab before
dinner. It was at this point that he began to cut
corners with disastrous results. Amberley Royal
station being five miles away, and putting in of
horses a matter of time, Wilton had told Howard,
the immaculate butler, to signal the next train to
stop; and Howard, who was more of a man of re-
source than his master gave him credit for, had, with
the red flag of the ninth hole of the links which
crossed the bottom of the lawn, signalled vehemently to the first down-train; and it had stopped.
Here Wilton's account became confused. He attempted, it seems, to get into that highly indignant
express, but a guard restrained him with more or
less force — hauled him, in fact, backwards from
the window of a locked carriage. Wilton must
have struck the gravel with some vehemence, for
the consequences, he admitted, were a free fight
on the line, in which he lost his hat, and was at

last dragged into the guard's van and set down breathless.

He had pressed money upon the man, and very foolishly had explained everything but his name. This he clung to, for he had a vision of tall head-lines in the New York papers, and well knew no son of Merton Sargent could expect mercy that side the water. The guard, to Wilton's amazement, refused the money on the grounds that this was a matter for the Company to attend to. Wilton insisted on his incognito, and, therefore, found two policemen waiting for him at St. Botolph terminus. When he expressed a wish to buy a new hat and telegraph to his friends, both policemen with one voice warned him that whatever he said would be used as evidence against him; and this had impressed Wilton tremendously.

"They were so infernally polite," he said. "If they had clubbed me I wouldn't have cared; but it was, 'Step this way, sir,' and, 'Up those stairs, please, sir,' till they jailed me — jailed me like a common drunk, and I had to stay in a filthy little cubby-hole of a cell all night."

"That comes of not giving your name and not wiring your lawyer," I replied. "What did you get?"

"Forty shillings, or a month," said Wilton, promptly — "next morning bright and early. They were working us off, three a minute. A

girl in a pink hat — she was brought in at three
in the morning — got ten days. I suppose I was
lucky. I must have knocked his senses out of
the guard. He told the old duck on the bench
that I had told him I was a sergeant in the
army, and that I was gathering beetles on the
track. *That* comes of trying to explain to an
Englishman."

" And you ? "

" Oh, I said nothing. I wanted to get out. I
paid my fine, and bought a new hat, and came up
here before noon next morning. There were a lot
of people in the house, and I told 'em I'd been
unavoidably detained, and then they began to
recollect engagements elsewhere. Hackman must
have seen the fight on the track and made a story
of it. I suppose they thought it was distinctly
American — confound 'em! It's the only time
in my life that I've ever flagged a train, and I
wouldn't have done it but for that scarab. 'T
wouldn't hurt their old trains to be held up once
in a while."

" Well, it's all over now," I said, choking a
little. " And your name didn't get into the papers. It *is* rather transatlantic when you come
to think of it."

" Over ! " Wilton grunted savagely. " It's only
just begun. That trouble with the guard was
just common, ordinary assault — merely a little

criminal business. The flagging of the train is civil — infernally civil — and means something quite different. They're after me for that now."

" Who ? "

" The Great Buchonian. There was a man in court watching the case on behalf of the Company. I gave him my name in a quiet corner before I bought my hat, and — come to dinner now; I'll show you the results afterwards."

The telling of his wrongs had worked Wilton Sargent into a very fine temper, and I do not think that my conversation soothed him. In the course of the dinner, prompted by a devil of pure mischief, I dwelt with loving insistence on certain smells and sounds of New York which go straight to the heart of the native in foreign parts; and Wilton began to ask many questions about his associates aforetime — men of the New York Yacht Club, Storm King, or the Restigouche, owners of rivers, ranches, and shipping in their playtime, lords of railways, kerosene, wheat, and cattle in their offices. When the green mint came, I gave him a peculiarly oily and atrocious cigar, of the brand they sell in the tessellated, electric-lighted, with-expensive-pictures-of-the-nude-adorned bar of the Pandemonium, and Wilton chewed the end for several minutes ere he lit it. The butler left us alone, and the chimney of the oak-panelled dining-room began to smoke.

" That's another ! " said he, poking the fire savagely, and I knew what he meant. One cannot put steam-heat in houses where Queen Elizabeth slept. The steady beat of a night-mail, whirling down the valley, recalled me to business. " What about the Great Buchonian ? " I said.

" Come into my study. That's all — as yet."

It was a pile of Seidlitz-powders-coloured correspondence, perhaps nine inches high, and it looked very businesslike.

" You can go through it," said Wilton. " Now I could take a chair and a red flag and go into Hyde Park and say the most atrocious things about your Queen, and preach anarchy and all that, y' know, till I was hoarse, and no one would take any notice. The Police — damn 'em ! — would protect me if I got into trouble. But for a little thing like flagging a dirty little sawed-off train — running through my own grounds, too — I get the whole British Constitution down on me as if I sold bombs. I don't understand it."

" No more does the Great Buchonian — apparently." I was turning over the letters. " Here's the traffic superintendent writing that it's utterly incomprehensible that any man should . . . Good heavens, Wilton, you *have* done it!" I giggled, as I read on.

" What's funny now ? " said my host.

" It seems that you, or Howard for you, stopped the three-forty Northern down."

" I ought to know that! They all had their knife into me, from the engine-driver up."

" But it's *the* three-forty — the Induna — surely you've heard of the Great Buchonian's Induna!"

" How the deuce am I to know one train from another? They come along about every two minutes."

" Quite so. But this happens to be the Induna — *the* one train of the whole line. She's timed for fifty-seven miles an hour. She was put on early in the Sixties, and she has never been stopped — "

" *I* know! Since William the Conqueror came over, or King Charles hid in her smoke-stack. You're as bad as the rest of these Britishers. If she's been run all that while, it's time she was flagged once or twice."

The American was beginning to ooze out all over Wilton, and his small-boned hands were moving restlessly.

" Suppose you flagged the Empire State Express, or the Western Cyclone? "

" Suppose I did. I know Otis Harvey — or used to. I'd send him a wire, and he'd understand it was a ground-hog case with me. That's exactly what I told this British fossil company here."

" Have you been answering their letters without legal advice, then? "

" Of course I have."

" Oh, my Sainted Country ! Go ahead, Wilton."

" I wrote 'em that I'd be very happy to see their president and explain to him in three words all about it; but that wouldn't do. 'Seems their president must be a god. He was too busy, and — well, you can read for yourself — they wanted explanations. The station-master at Amberley Royal — and he grovels before me, as a rule — wanted an explanation, and quick, too. The head sachem at St. Botolph's wanted three or four, and the Lord High Mukkamuk that oils the locomotives wanted one every fine day. I told 'em — I've told 'em about fifty times — I stopped their holy and sacred train because I wanted to board her. Did they think I wanted to feel her pulse ? "

" You didn't say that ? "

" ' Feel her pulse ' ? Of course not."

" No. ' Board her.' "

" What else could I say ? "

" My dear Wilton, what *is* the use of Mrs. Sherborne, and the Clays, and all that lot working over you for four years to make an Englishman out of you, if the very first time you're rattled you go back to the vernacular ? "

" I'm through with Mrs. Sherborne and the rest of the crowd. America's good enough for me. What ought I to have said ? ' Please,' or ' thanks awf'ly,' or how ? "

There was no chance now of mistaking the

man's nationality. Speech, gesture, and step, so carefully drilled into him, had gone away with the borrowed mask of indifference. It was a lawful son of the Youngest People, whose predecessors were the Red Indian. His voice had risen to the high, throaty crow of his breed when they labour under excitement. His close-set eyes showed by turns unnecessary fear, annoyance beyond reason, rapid and purposeless flights of thought, the child's lust for immediate revenge, and the child's pathetic bewilderment, who knocks his head against the bad, wicked table. And on the other side, I knew, stood the Company, as unable as Wilton to understand.

"And I could buy their old road three times over," he muttered, playing with a paper-knife, and moving restlessly to and fro.

"You didn't tell 'em *that*, I hope!"

There was no answer; but as I went through the letters, I felt that Wilton must have told them many surprising things. The Great Buchonian had first asked for an explanation of the stoppage of their Induna, and had found a certain levity in the explanation tendered. It then advised "Mr. W. Sargent" to refer his solicitor to their solicitor, or whatever the legal phrase is.

"And you didn't?" I said, looking up.

"No. They were treating me exactly as if I had been a kid playing on the cable-tracks. There was not the *least* necessity for any solicitor. Five minutes' quiet talk would have settled everything."

I returned to the correspondence. The Great Buchonian regretted that, owing to pressure of business, none of their directors could accept Mr. W. Sargent's invitation to run down and discuss the difficulty. The Great Buchonian was careful to point out that no animus underlay their action, nor was money their object. Their duty was to protect the interests of their line, and these interests could not be protected if a precedent were established whereby any of the Queen's subjects could stop a train in mid-career. Again (this was another branch of the correspondence, not more than five heads of departments being concerned), the Company admitted that there was some reasonable doubt as to the duties of express-trains in all crises, and the matter was open to settlement by process of law till an authoritative ruling was obtained — from the House of Lords, if necessary.

"That broke me all up," said Wilton, who was reading over my shoulder. "I knew I'd struck the British Constitution at last. The House of Lords — my Lord! And, anyway, I'm not one of the Queen's subjects."

"Why, I had a notion that you'd got yourself naturalised."

Wilton blushed hotly as he explained that very

169

many things must happen to the British Constitution ere he took out his papers.

"How does it all strike you?" he said. "Isn't the Great Buchonian crazy?"

"I don't know. You've done something that no one ever thought of doing before, and the Company don't know what to make of it. I see they offer to send down their solicitor and another official of the Company to talk things over informally. Then here's another letter suggesting that you put up a fourteen-foot wall, crowned with bottle-glass, at the bottom of the garden."

"Talk of British insolence! The man who recommends *that* (he's another bloated functionary) says that I shall 'derive great pleasure from watching the wall going up day by day'! Did you ever dream of such gall? I've offered 'em money enough to buy a new set of cars and pension the driver for three generations; but that doesn't seem to be what they want. They expect me to go to the House of Lords and get a ruling, and build walls between times. Are they *all* stark, raving mad? One 'ud think I made a profession of flagging trains. How in Tophet was I to know their old Induna from a way-train? I took the first that came along, and I've been jailed and fined for that once already."

"That was for slugging the guard."

"He had no right to haul me out when I was half-way through a window."

170

" What are you going to do about it ? "

" Their lawyer and the other official (can't they trust their men unless they send 'em in pairs ?) are coming here to-night. I told 'em I was busy, as a rule, till after dinner, but they might send along the entire directorate if it eased 'em any."

Now, after-dinner visiting, for business or pleasure, is the custom of the smaller American town, and not that of England, where the end of the day is sacred to the owner, not the public. Verily, Wilton Sargent had hoisted the striped flag of rebellion!

" Isn't it time that the humour of the situation began to strike you, Wilton ? " I asked.

" Where's the humour of baiting an American citizen just because he happens to be a millionaire—poor devil?" He was silent for a little time, and then went on: " Of course. *Now* I see!" He spun round and faced me excitedly. " It's as plain as mud. These ducks are laying their pipes to skin me."

" They say explicitly they don't want money! "

" That's all a blind. So's their addressing me as W. Sargent. They know well enough who I am. They know I'm the old man's son. Why didn't I think of that before ? "

" One minute, Wilton. If you climbed to the top of the dome of St. Paul's and offered a reward to any Englishman who could tell you who or what Merton Sargent had been, there wouldn't be twenty men in all London to claim it."

"That's their insular provincialism, then. I don't care a cent. The old man would have wrecked the Great Buchonian before breakfast for a pipe-opener. My God, I'll do it in dead earnest! I'll show 'em that they can't bulldoze a foreigner for flagging one of their little tin-pot trains, and — I've spent fifty thousand a year here, at least, for the last four years."

I was glad I was not his lawyer. I re-read the correspondence, notably the letter which recommended him — almost tenderly, I fancied — to build a fourteen-foot brick wall at the end of his garden, and half-way through it a thought struck me which filled me with pure joy.

The footman ushered in two men, frock-coated, grey-trousered, smooth-shaven, heavy of speech and gait. It was nearly nine o'clock, but they looked as newly come from a bath. I could not understand why the elder and taller of the pair glanced at me as though we had an understanding; nor why he shook hands with an un-English warmth.

"This simplifies the situation," he said in an undertone, and, as I stared, he whispered to his companion: "I fear I shall be of very little service at present. Perhaps Mr. Folsom had better talk over the affair with Mr. Sargent."

" That is what I am here for," said Wilton.

The man of law smiled pleasantly, and said that he saw no reason why the difficulty should not be arranged in two minutes' quiet talk. His air, as he sat down opposite Wilton, was soothing to the last degree, and his companion drew me up-stage. The mystery was deepening, but I followed meekly, and heard Wilton say, with an uneasy laugh :

" I've had insomnia over this affair, Mr. Folsom. Let's settle it one way or the other, for heaven's sake ! "

" Ah ! Has he suffered much from this lately ? " said my man, with a preliminary cough.

" I really can't say," I replied.

" Then I suppose you have only lately taken charge here ? "

" I came this evening. I am not exactly in charge of anything."

" I see. Merely to observe the course of events in case — " He nodded.

" Exactly." Observation, after all, is my trade. He coughed again slightly, and came to business.

" Now — I am asking solely for information's sake — do you find the delusions persistent ? "

" Which delusions ? "

" They are variable, then ? That is distinctly curious, because — but do I understand that the *type* of the delusion varies? For example, Mr. Sargent believes that he can buy the Great Buchonian."

"Did he write you that?"

"He made the offer to the Company — on a half-sheet of notepaper. Now, has he by chance gone to the other extreme, and believed that he is in danger of becoming a pauper? The curious economy in the use of a half-sheet of paper shows that some idea of that kind might have flashed through his mind, and the two delusions can coexist, but it is not common. As you must know, the delusion of vast wealth — the folly of grandeurs, I believe our friends the French call it — is, as a rule, persistent, to the exclusion of all others."

Then I heard Wilton's best English voice at the end of the study:

"My *dear* sir, I have explained twenty times already, I wanted to get that scarab in time for dinner. Suppose you had left an important legal document in the same way?"

"That touch of cunning is very significant," my fellow-practitioner — since he insisted on it — muttered.

"I am very happy, of course, to meet you; but if you had only sent your president down to dinner here, I could have settled the thing in half a minute. Why, I could have bought the Buchonian

from him while your clerks were sending me this."
Wilton dropped his hand heavily on the blue-and-
white correspondence, and the lawyer started.

"But, speaking frankly," the lawyer replied, "it
is, if I may say so, perfectly inconceivable, even in
the case of the most important legal documents,
that any one should stop the three-forty express —
the Induna — Our Induna, my dear sir."

"Absolutely!" my companion echoed; then to
me in a lower tone: "You notice, again, the persistent delusion of wealth. *I* was called in when
he wrote us that. You can see it is utterly impossible for the Company to continue to run their
trains through the property of a man who may at
any moment fancy himself divinely commissioned
to stop all traffic. If he had only referred us to
his lawyer — but, naturally, *that* he would not do,
under the circumstances. A pity — a great pity.
He is so young. By the way, it is curious, is it
not, to note the absolute conviction in the voice
of those who are similarly afflicted — heartrending,
I might say — and the inability to follow a chain
of connected thought."

"I can't see what you want," Wilton was saying
to the lawyer.

"It need not be more than fourteen feet high —
a really desirable structure, and it would be possible to grow pear-trees on the sunny side." The
lawyer was speaking in an unprofessional voice.

175

"There are few things pleasanter than to watch, so to say, one's own vine and fig-tree in full bearing. Consider the profit and amusement you would derive from it. If *you* could see your way to doing this, *we* could arrange all the details with your lawyer, and it is possible that the Company might bear some of the cost. I have put the matter, I trust, in a nutshell. If you, my dear sir, will interest yourself in building that wall, and will kindly give us the name of your lawyer, I dare assure you that you will hear no more from the Great Buchonian."

"But why am I to disfigure my lawn with a new brick wall?"

"Grey flint is extremely picturesque."

"Grey flint, then, if you put it that way. Why the dickens must I go building towers of Babylon just because I have held up one of your trains — once?"

"The expression he used in his third letter was that he wished to 'board her,'" said my companion in my ear. "That was very curious — a marine delusion impinging, as it were, upon a land one. What a marvellous world he must move in — and will before the curtain falls. So young, too — so very young!"

"Well, if you want the plain English of it, I'm damned if I go wall-building to your orders. You can fight it all along the line, into the House of

Lords and out again, and get your rulings by the running foot if you like," said Wilton, hotly. "Great heavens, man, I only did it once!"

"We have at present no guarantee that you may not do it again; and, with our traffic, we must, in justice to our passengers, demand some form of guarantee. It must not serve as a precedent. All this might have been saved if you had only referred us to your legal representative." The lawyer looked appealingly around the room. The dead-lock was complete.

"Wilton," I asked, "may I try my hand now?"

"Anything you like," said Wilton. "It seems I can't talk English. I won't build any wall, though." He threw himself back in his chair.

"Gentlemen," I said deliberately, for I perceived that the doctor's mind would turn slowly, "Mr. Sargent has very large interests in the chief railway systems of his own country."

"His own country?" said the lawyer.

"At that age?" said the doctor.

"Certainly. He inherited them from his father, Mr. Sargent, who was an American."

"And proud of it," said Wilton, as though he had been a Western Senator let loose on the Continent for the first time.

"My dear sir," said the lawyer, half rising, "why did you not acquaint the Company with this fact —

this vital fact — early in our correspondence? We should have understood. We should have made allowances."

"Allowances be damned. Am I a Red Indian or a lunatic?"

The two men looked guilty.

"If Mr. Sargent's friend had told us as much in the beginning," said the doctor, very severely, "much might have been saved." Alas! I had made a life's enemy of that doctor.

"I hadn't a chance," I replied. "Now, of course, you can see that a man who owns several thousand miles of line, as Mr. Sargent does, would be apt to treat railways a shade more casually than other people."

"Of course; of course. He is an American; that accounts. Still, it *was* the Induna; but I can quite understand that the customs of our cousins across the water differ in these particulars from ours. And do you always stop trains in this way in the States, Mr. Sargent?"

"I should if occasion ever arose; but I've never had to yet. Are you going to make an international complication of the business?"

"You need give yourself no further concern whatever in the matter. We see that there is no likelihood of this action of yours establishing a precedent, which was the only thing we were afraid of. Now that you understand that we cannot reconcile our system to any sudden stoppages, we feel quite sure that — "

" I sha'n't be staying long enough to flag another train," Wilton said pensively.

" You are returning, then, to our fellow-kinsmen across the — ah — big pond, you call it ? "

" *No*, sir. The ocean — the North Atlantic Ocean. It's three thousand miles broad, and three miles deep in places. I wish it were ten thousand."

" I am not so fond of sea-travel myself; but I think it is every Englishman's duty once in his life to study the great branch of our Anglo-Saxon race across the ocean," said the lawyer.

" If ever you come over, and care to flag any train on my system, I'll — I'll see you through," said Wilton.

" Thank you — ah, thank you. You're very kind. I'm sure I should enjoy myself immensely."

" We have overlooked the fact," the doctor whispered to me, " that your friend proposed to buy the Great Buchonian."

" He is worth anything from twenty to thirty million dollars — four to five million pounds," I answered, knowing that it would be hopeless to explain.

" Really ! That is enormous wealth. But the Great Buchonian is not in the market."

" Perhaps he does not want to buy it now."

"It would be impossible under any circumstances," said the doctor.

"How characteristic!" murmured the lawyer, reviewing matters in his mind. "I always understood from books that your countrymen were in a hurry. And so you would have gone forty miles to town and back — before dinner — to get a scarab? How intensely American! But you talk exactly like an Englishman, Mr. Sargent."

"That is a fault that can be remedied. There's only one question I'd like to ask you. You said it was inconceivable that any man should stop a train on your road?"

"And so it is — absolutely inconceivable."

"Any sane man, that is?"

"That is what I meant, of course. I mean, with excep — "

"Thank you."

The two men departed. Wilton checked himself as he was about to fill a pipe, took one of my cigars instead, and was silent for fifteen minutes.

Then said he : "Have you got a list of the Southampton sailings on you?"

* * * * * * * * * *

Far away from the greystone wings, the dark cedars, the faultless gravel drives, and the mint-sauce lawns of Holt Hangars runs a river called the Hudson, whose unkempt banks are covered with the palaces of those wealthy beyond the dreams of avarice. Here, where the hoot of the Haverstraw brick-barge-tug answers the howl of the locomotive on either shore, you shall find, with a complete installation of electric light, nickel-plated binnacles, and a calliope attachment to her steam-whistle, the twelve-hundred-ton ocean-going steam-yacht *Columbia*, lying at her private pier, to take to his office, at an average speed of seventeen knots an hour — and the barges can look out for themselves — Wilton Sargent, American.

THE RECORD OF BADALIA
HERODSFOOT

THE RECORD OF BADALIA
HERODSFOOT [1]

The year's at the spring
And day's at the dawn ;
Morning's at seven ;
The hillside's dew-pearled ;
The lark's on the wing ;
The snail's on the thorn :
God's in his heaven —
All's right with the world!

Pippa Passes.

THIS is not that Badalia whose spare names were
Joanna, Pugnacious, and M'Canna, as the song
says, but another and much nicer lady.

In the beginning of things she had been unregenerate; had worn the heavy fluffy fringe which
is the ornament of the costermonger's girl, and
there is a legend in Gunnison Street that on her
wedding-day she, a flare-lamp in either hand,
danced dances on a discarded lover's winkle-barrow,
till a policeman interfered, and then Badalia danced
with the Law amid shoutings. Those were her
days of fatness, and they did not last long, for her

husband after two years took to himself another woman, and passed out of Badalia's life, over Badalia's senseless body; for he stifled protest with blows. While she was enjoying her widowhood the baby that the husband had not taken away died of croup, and Badalia was altogether alone. With rare fidelity she listened to no proposals for a second marriage according to the customs of Gunnison Street, which do not differ from those of the Barralong. "My man," she explained to her suitors, "'e'll come back one o' these days, an' then, like as not, 'e'll take an' kill me if I was livin' 'long o' you. You don't know Tom; I do. Now you go. I can do for myself — not 'avin' a kid." She did for herself with a mangle, some tending of babies, and an occasional sale of flowers. This latter trade is one that needs capital, and takes the vendor very far westward, insomuch that the return journey from, let us say, the Burlington Arcade to Gunnison Street, E., is an excuse for drink, and then, as Badalia pointed out, "You come 'ome with your shawl 'arf off of your back, an' your bonnick under your arm, and the price of nothing-at-all in your pocket, let alone a slop takin' care o' you." Badalia did not drink, but she knew her sisterhood, and gave them rude counsel. Otherwise she kept herself to herself, and meditated a great deal upon Tom Herodsfoot, her husband, who would come back some day, and the baby that would never return. In what manner these thoughts wrought upon her mind will not be known.

Her entry into society dates from the night when she rose literally under the feet of the Reverend Eustace Hanna, on the landing of No. 17 Gunnison Street, and told him that he was a fool, without discernment in the dispensation of his district charities.

"You give Lascar Loo custids," said she, without the formality of introduction; "give her porkwine. Garn! Give 'er blankits. Garn 'ome! Er mother, she eats 'em all, and drinks the blankits. 'Gits 'em back from the shop, she does, before you come visiting again, so as to 'ave 'em all handy an' proper; an' Lascar Loo she sez to you, 'Oh, my mother's that good to me!' she do. Lascar Loo 'ad better talk so, bein' sick abed, 'r else 'er mother would kill 'er. Garn! you're a bloomin' gardener —you an' yer custids! Lascar Loo don't never smell of 'em even."

Thereon the curate, instead of being offended, recognised in the heavy eyes under the fringe the soul of a fellow-worker, and so bade Badalia mount guard over Lascar Loo, when the next jelly or custard should arrive, to see that the invalid actually ate it. This Badalia did, to the disgust of Lascar Loo's mother, and the sharing of a black eye between the three; but Lascar Loo got her custard, and coughing heartily, rather enjoyed the fray.

Later on, partly through the Reverend Eustace Hanna's swift recognition of her uses, and partly through certain tales poured out with moist eyes and flushed cheeks by Sister Eva, youngest and most impressionable of the Little Sisters of the Red Diamond, it came to pass that Badalia, arrogant, fluffy-fringed, and perfectly unlicensed in speech, won a recognised place among such as labour in Gunnison Street.

These were a mixed corps, zealous or hysterical, faint-hearted or only very wearied of battle against misery, according to their lights. The most part were consumed with small rivalries and personal jealousies, to be retailed confidentially to their own tiny cliques in the pauses between wrestling with death for the body of a moribund laundress, or scheming for further mission-grants to resole a consumptive compositor's very consumptive boots. There was a rector that lived in dread of pauperising the poor, would fain have held bazaars for fresh altar-cloths, and prayed in secret for a new large brass bird, with eyes of red glass, fondly believed to be carbuncles. There was Brother Victor, of the Order of Little Ease, who knew a great deal about altar-cloths but kept his knowledge in the background while he strove to propitiate Mrs. Jessel, the Secretary of the Tea Cup Board, who had money to dispense but hated Rome — even though Rome would, on its honour, do no more than fill the stomach, leaving the dazed soul to the mercies of Mrs. Jessel. There were all the Little Sisters of the Red Diamond, daughters of the horse-leech, crying " Give " when their own charity was exhausted, and pitifully explaining to such as demanded an account of their disbursements in return for one half-sovereign, that relief-work in a bad district can hardly be systematised on the accounts' side without expensive duplication of staff. There was the Reverend Eustace Hanna, who worked impartially with Ladies' Committees, Androgynous Leagues and Guilds, Brother Victor, and anybody else who could give him money, boots, or blankets, or that more precious help that allows itself to be directed by those who know. And all these people learned, one by one, to consult Badalia on matters of personal character, right to relief, and hope of eventual reformation in Gunnison Street. Her answers were seldom cheering, but she possessed special knowledge and complete confidence in herself.

" I'm Gunnison Street," she said to the austere Mrs. Jessel. " I know what's what, *I* do, an' they don't want your religion, Mum, not a single ——. Excuse me. It's all right when they comes to die, Mum, but till they die what they wants is things to eat. The men they'll shif' for themselves. That's why Nick Lapworth sez to you that 'e wants to be confirmed an' all that. 'E won't never lead no new life, nor 'is wife won't get no good out o' all the money you gives 'im. No more you can't pauperise them as 'asn't things to begin with. They're bloomin' well pauped! The women they can't shif' for themselves — 'specially bein' always confined. 'Ow should they? They wants things if they can get 'em anyways. If not they dies, and a good job too, for women is cruel put upon in Gunnison Street."

"Do you believe that — that Mrs. Herodsfoot is altogether a proper person to trust funds to?" said Mrs. Jessel to the curate after this conversation. "She seems to be utterly godless in her speech at least."

The curate agreed. She was godless according to Mrs. Jessel's views, but did not Mrs. Jessel think that since Badalia knew Gunnison Street and its needs, as none other knew it, she might in a humble way be, as it were, the scullion of charity from purer sources, and that if, say, the Tea Cup Board could give a few shillings a week, and the Little Sisters of the Red Diamond a few more, and, yes, he himself could raise yet a few more, the total, not at all likely to be excessive, might be handed over to Badalia to dispense among her associates. Thus Mrs. Jessel herself would be set free to attend more directly to the spiritual wants of certain large-limbed hulking men who sat picturesquely on the lower benches of her gatherings and sought for truth — which is quite as precious as silver, when you know the market for it.

" She'll favour her own friends," said Mrs. Jessel. The curate refrained from mirth, and, after wise flattery, carried his point. To her unbounded pride Badalia was appointed the dispenser of a grant — a weekly trust, to be held for the benefit of Gunnison Street.

" I don't know what we can get together each week," said the curate to her. " But here are seventeen shillings to start with. You do what you like with them among your people, only let me know how it goes so that we sha'n't get muddled in the accounts. D' you see ? "

"Ho, yuss! 'Tain't much, though, is it ? " said Badalia, regarding the white coins in her palm. The sacred fever of the administrator, only known to those who have tasted power, burned in her veins. " Boots is boots, unless they're give you, an' then they ain't fit to wear unless they're mended top an' bottom; an' jellies is jellies; an' I don't think anything o' that cheap pork-wine, but it all comes to something. It'll go quicker'n a quartern of gin — seventeen bob. An' I'll keep a book — same as I used to do before Tom went an' took up 'long o' that pan-faced slut in

Hennessy's Rents. We was the only barrer that kep' regular books, me an' — 'im."

She bought a large copy-book — her unschooled handwriting demanded room — and in it she wrote the story of her war; boldly, as befits a general, and for no other eyes than her own and those of the Reverend Eustace Hanna. Long ere the pages were full the mottled cover had been soaked in kerosene — Lascar Loo's mother, defrauded of her percentage on her daughter's custards, invaded Badalia's room in 17 Gunnison Street, and fought with her to the damage of the lamp and her own hair. It was hard, too, to carry the precious "pork-wine" in one hand and the book in the other through an eternally thirsty land; so red stains were added to those of the oil. But the Reverend Eustace Hanna, looking at the matter of the book, never objected. The generous scrawls told their own tale, Badalia every Saturday night supplying the chorus between the written statements thus:—

Mrs. Hikkey, very ill brandy 3*d. Cab for hospital, she had to go,* 1*s. Mrs. Poone confined. In money for tea (she took it I know, sir)* 6*d. Met her husband out looking for work.*

"I slapped 'is face for a bone-idle beggar! 'E won't get no work this side o'—excuse me, sir. Won't you go on?" The curate continued—

Mrs. Vincent. Confid. No linning for baby.

Most untidy. In money 2s. 6d. *Some clothes from Miss Evva.*

"Did Sister Eva do that?" said the curate, very softly. Now charity was Sister Eva's bounden duty, yet to one man's eyes each act of her daily toil was a manifestation of angelic grace and goodness — a thing to perpetually admire.

"Yes, sir. She went back to the Sisters' 'Ome an' took 'em off 'er own bed. Most beautiful marked too. Go on, sir. That makes up four and thruppence."

Mrs. Junnet to keep good fire coals is up. 7d.

Mrs. Lockhart took a baby to nurse to earn a trifle but mother can'd pay husband summons over and over. He won't help. Cash 2s. 2d. *Worked in a ketchin but had to leave. Fire, tea, and shin of beef* 1s. 7½d.

"There was a fight there, sir," said Badalia. "Not me, sir. 'Er 'usband, o' course 'e come in at the wrong time, was wishful to 'ave the beef, so I calls up the next floor, an' down comes that mulatter man wot sells the sword-stick canes, top o' Ludgate-'ill. 'Muley,' sez I, 'you big black beast, you, take an' kill this big white beast 'ere.' I knew I couldn't stop Tom Lockart 'alf drunk, with the beef in 'is 'ands. 'I'll beef 'm,' sez Muley, an' 'e did it, with that pore woman a-cryin' in the next room, an' the top banisters on that landin' is broke out, but she got 'er beef-tea, an' Tom 'e's got 'is gruel. Will you go on, sir?"

"No, I think it will be all right. I'll sign for the week," said the curate. One gets so used to these things profanely called human documents.

"Mrs. Churner's baby's got diptheery," said Badalia, turning to go.

"Where's that? The Churners of Painter's Alley, or the other Churners in Houghton Street?"

"Houghton Street. The Painter's Alley people, they're sold an' left."

"Sister Eva's sitting one night a week with old Mrs. Probyn in Houghton Street — isn't she?" said the curate, uneasily.

"Yes; but she won't sit no longer. *I've* took up Mrs. Probyn. I can't talk 'er no religion, but she don't want it; an' Miss Eva she don't want no diptheery, tho' she sez she does. Don't *you* be afraid for Miss Eva."

"But — but you'll get it, perhaps."

"Like as not." She looked the curate between the eyes, and her own eyes flamed under the fringe. "Maybe I'd like to get it, for aught you know."

The curate thought upon these words for a little time till he began to think of Sister Eva in the grey cloak with the white bonnet ribbons under the chin. Then he thought no more of Badalia.

What Badalia thought was never expressed in words, but it is known in Gunnison Street that

Lascar Loo's mother, sitting blind-drunk on her own door-step, was that night captured and wrapped up in the war-cloud of Badalia's wrath, so that she did not know whether she stood on her head or her heels, and after being soundly bumped on every particular stair up to her room, was set down on Badalia's bed, there to whimper and quiver till the dawn, protesting that all the world was against her, and calling on the names of children long since slain by dirt and neglect. Badalia, snorting, went out to war, and since the hosts of the enemy were many, found enough work to keep her busy till the dawn.

As she had promised, she took Mrs. Probyn into her own care, and began by nearly startling the old lady into a fit with the announcement that "there ain't no God like as not, an' if there *is* it don't matter to you or me, an' any'ow you take this jelly." Sister Eva objected to being shut off from her pious work in Houghton Street, but Badalia insisted, and by fair words and the promise of favours to come so prevailed on three or four of the more sober men of the neighbourhood that they blockaded the door whenever Sister Eva attempted to force an entry, and pleaded the diphtheria as an excuse. "I've got to keep 'er out o' 'arm's way," said Badalia, "an' out she keeps. The curick won't care a —— for me, but — 'e wouldn't any'ow."

The effect of that quarantine was to shift the sphere of Sister Eva's activity to other streets, and notably those most haunted by the Reverend Eustace Hanna and Brother Victor, of the Order of Little Ease. There exists, for all their human bickerings, a very close brotherhood in the ranks of those whose work lies in Gunnison Street. To begin with, they have seen pain — pain that no word or deed of theirs can alleviate — life born into Death, and Death crowded down by unhappy life. Also they understand the full significance of drink, which is a knowledge hidden from very many well-meaning people, and some of them have fought with the beasts at Ephesus. They meet at unseemly hours in unseemly places, exchange a word or two of hasty counsel, advice, or suggestion, and pass on to their appointed toil, since time is precious and lives hang in the balance of five minutes. For many, the gas-lamps are their sun, and the Covent Garden wains the chariots of the twilight. They have all in their station begged for money, so that the freemasonry of the mendicant binds them together.

To all these influences there was added in the case of two workers that thing which men have agreed to call Love. The chance of Sister Eva's catching diphtheria did not enter into the curate's head till Badalia had spoken. Then it seemed a thing intolerable and monstrous that she should be exposed not only to this risk, but any accident whatever of the streets. A wain coming round a corner might kill her; the rotten staircases on which she trod daily and nightly might collapse and maim her; there was danger in the tottering coping-stones of certain crazy houses that he knew well; danger more deadly within those houses. What if one of a thousand drunken men crushed out that precious life? A woman had once flung a chair at the curate's head. Sister Eva's arm would not be strong enough to ward off a chair. There were also knives that were apt to fly. These and other considerations cast the soul of the Reverend Eustace Hanna into torment, that no leaning upon Providence could relieve. God was indubitably great and terrible — one had only to walk through Gunnison Street to see that much — but it would be better, vastly better, that Eva should have the protection of his own arm. And the world that was not too busy to watch might have seen a woman, not too young, light-haired and light-eyed, slightly assertive in her speech, and very limited in such ideas as lay beyond the immediate sphere of her duty, where the eyes of the Reverend Eustace Hanna turned to follow the footsteps of a Queen crowned in a little grey bonnet with white ribbons under the chin.

If that bonnet appeared for a moment at the bottom of a court-yard, or nodded at him on a dark staircase, then there was hope yet for Lascar Loo, living on one lung and the memory of past excesses, hope even for whining sodden Nick Lapworth, blaspheming in the hope of money over the pangs of a "true conversion this time, s' 'elp me Gawd, sir." If that bonnet did not appear for a day, the mind of the curate was filled with lively pictures of horror, visions of stretchers, a crowd at some villainous crossing, and a policeman — he could see that policeman — jerking out over his shoulder the details of the accident, and ordering the man who would have set his body against the wheels — heavy dray-wheels, he could see them — to "move on." Then there was less hope for the salvation of Gunnison Street and all in it.

This agony Brother Victor beheld one day when he was coming from a death-bed. He saw the light in the eye, the relaxing muscles of the mouth, and heard a new ring in the voice that had told flat all the forenoon. Sister Eva had turned into Gunnison Street after a forty-eight hours' eternity of absence. She had not been run over. Brother Victor's heart must have suffered in some human fashion, or he would never have seen what he saw. But the Law of his Church made suffering easy. His duty was to go on with his work until he died, even as Badalia went on. She, magnifying her office, faced the drunken husband; coaxed the doubly shiftless, thriftless girl-wife into a little forethought, and begged clothes when and where she could for the scrofulous babes that multiplied like the green scum on the untopped water-cisterns.

The story of her deeds was written in the book that the curate signed weekly, but she never told him any more of fights and tumults in the street. "Mis' Eva does 'er work 'er way. I does mine mine. But I do more than Mis' Eva ten times over, an' 'Thank yer, Badalia,' sez 'e, 'that'll do for this week.' I wonder what Tom's doin' now 'long o' that — other woman. 'Seems like as if I'd go an' look at 'im one o' these days. But I'd cut 'er liver out—couldn't 'elp myself. Better not go, p'r'aps."

Hennessy's Rents lay more than two miles from Gunnison Street, and were inhabited by much the same class of people. Tom had established himself there with Jenny Wabstow, his new woman, and for weeks lived in great fear of Badalia's suddenly descending upon him. The prospect of actual fighting did not scare him: but he objected to the police-court that would follow, and the orders for maintenance and other devices of a law that cannot understand the simple rule that "when a man's tired of a woman 'e ain't such a bloomin' fool as to live with 'er no more, an' that's the long an' short of it." For some months his new wife wore very well, and kept Tom in a state of decent fear and consequent orderliness. Also work was plentiful. Then a baby was born, and, following the law of his kind, Tom, little interested in the children he helped to produce, sought distraction in drink. He had confined himself, as a rule, to beer, which is stupefying and comparatively innocuous: at least, it clogs the legs, and though the heart may ardently desire to kill, sleep comes swiftly, and the crime often remains undone. Spirits, being more volatile, allow both the flesh and the soul to work together — generally to the inconvenience of others. Tom discovered that there was merit in whisky — if you only took enough of it — cold. He took as much as he could purchase or get given him, and by the time that his woman was fit to go abroad again, the two rooms of their household were stripped of many valuable articles. Then the woman spoke her mind, not once, but several times, with point, fluency, and metaphor; and Tom was indignant at being deprived of peace at the end of his day's work, which included much whisky. He therefore withdrew himself from the solace and companionship of Jenny Wabstow, and she therefore pursued him with more metaphors. At the last, Tom would turn round and hit her — sometimes across the head, and sometimes across the breast, and the bruises furnished material for discussion on door-steps among such women as had been treated in like manner by their husbands. They were not few.

But no very public scandal had occurred till Tom one day saw fit to open negotiations with a young woman for matrimony according to the laws of free selection. He was getting very tired of Jenny, and the young woman was earning enough from flower-selling to keep him in comfort, whereas Jenny was expecting another baby and most unreasonably expected consideration on this account. The shapelessness of her figure revolted him, and he said as much in the language of his breed. Jenny cried till Mrs. Hart, lineal descendant, and Irish of the "mother to Mike of the donkey-cart," stopped her on her own staircase and whispered: "God be good to you, Jenny, my woman, for I see how 'tis with you." Jenny wept more than ever, and gave Mrs. Hart a penny and some kisses, while Tom was conducting his own wooing at the corner of the street.

The young woman, prompted by pride, not by virtue, told Jenny of his offers, and Jenny spoke to Tom that night. The altercation began in their own rooms, but Tom tried to escape; and in the end all Hennessy's Rents gathered themselves upon the pavement and formed a court to which Jenny appealed from time to time, her hair loose on her neck, her raiment in extreme disorder, and her steps astray from drink. "When your man drinks, you'd better drink too! It don't 'urt so much when 'e 'its you then," says the Wisdom of the Women. And surely they ought to know.

"Look at 'im!" shrieked Jenny. "Look at 'im, standin' there without any word to say for 'imself, that 'ud smitch off and leave me, an' never so much as a shillin' lef' be'ind! You call yourself a man — you call yourself the bleedin' shadow of a man? I've seen better men than you made outer chewed paper and sput out arterwards. Look at 'im! 'E's been drunk since Thursday last, an' 'e'll be drunk 's long 's 'e can get drink. 'E's took all I've got, an' me — an' me — as you see — "

A murmur of sympathy from the women.

"Took it all, 'e did, an' atop of 'is blasted pickin' an' stealin' — yes, you, you thief — 'e goes off an' tries to take up 'long o' that " — here followed a complete and minute description of the young woman. Luckily, she was not on the spot to hear. " 'E'll serve 'er as 'e served me! 'E'll drink every bloomin' copper she makes an' then leave 'er go, same as 'e done me! O women, look you, I've bore 'im one an' there's another on the way, an' 'e'd up an' leave me as I am now — the stinkin' dorg. An' you *may* leave me. I don't want none o' your leavin's. Go away. Get away!" The hoarseness of passion overpowered the voice. The crowd attracted a policeman as Tom began to slink away.

"Look at 'im," said Jenny, grateful for the new listener. "Ain't there no law for such as 'im? 'E's took all my money, 'e's beat me once, twice, an' over. 'E's swine-drunk when 'e ain't mad-drunk, an' now, an' now 'e's tryin' to pick up along o' another woman. 'Im I give up a four times better man for. Ain't there no law?"

"What's the matter now? You go into your 'ouse. I'll see to the man. 'As 'e been 'itting you?" said the policeman.

"'Ittin' me? 'E's cut my 'eart in two, an' 'e stands there grinnin' as tho' 'twas all a play to 'im."

"You go on into your 'ouse an' lie down a bit."

"I'm a married woman, I tell you, an' I'll 'ave my 'usband!"

"I ain't done 'er no bloomin' 'arm," said Tom from the edge of the crowd. He felt that public opinion was running against him.

"You ain't done me any bloomin' good, you dorg. I'm a married woman, I am, an' I won't 'ave my 'usband took from me."

"Well, if you are a married woman, cover your breasts," said the policeman, soothingly. He was used to domestic brawls.

"Sha'n't — thank you for your impidence. Look 'ere!" She tore open her dishevelled bodice and showed such crescent-shaped bruises as are made by a well-applied chair-back. "That's what

203

'e done to me acause my heart wouldn't break quick
enough! 'E's tried to get in an' break it. Look
at that, Tom, that you gave me last night; an' I
made it up with you. But that was before I
knew what you were tryin' to do 'long o' that
woman —"

"D' you charge 'im?" said the policeman.
"'E'll get a month for it, per'aps."

"No," said Jenny, firmly. It was one thing to
expose her man to the scorn of the street, and
another to lead him to jail.

"Then you go in an' lie down, and you"—
this to the crowd—"pass along the pavement,
there. Pass along. 'Tain't nothing to laugh at."
To Tom, who was being sympathised with by
his friends, "It's good for you she didn't charge
you, but mind this now, the next time," etc.

Tom did not at all appreciate Jenny's forbear-
ance, nor did his friends help to compose his mind.
He had whacked the woman because she was a
nuisance. For precisely the same reason he had
cast about for a new mate. And all his kind acts
had ended in a truly painful scene in the street,
a most unjustifiable exposure by and of his woman,
and a certain loss of caste — this he realised dimly
— among his associates. Consequently all women were nuisances, and consequently whisky
was a good thing. His friends condoled with
him. Perhaps he had been more hard on his

woman than she deserved, but her disgraceful conduct under provocation excused all offence.

" I wouldn't 'ave no more to do with 'er — a woman like that there," said one comforter.

" Let 'er go an' dig for her bloomin' self. A man wears 'isself out to 'is bones shovin' meat down their mouths, while they sit at 'ome easy all day ; an' the very fust time, mark you, you 'as a bit of a difference, an' very proper too for a man as *is* a man, she ups an' 'as you out into the street, callin' you Gawd knows what all. What's the good o' that, I arx you ? " So spoke the second comforter.

The whisky was the third, and his suggestion struck Tom as the best of all. He would return to Badalia, his wife. Probably she would have been doing something wrong while he had been away, and he could then vindicate his authority as a husband. Certainly she would have money. Single women always seemed to possess the pence that God and the Government denied to hard-working men. He refreshed himself with more whisky. It was beyond any doubt that Badalia would have done something wrong. She might even have married another man. He would wait till the new husband was out of the way, and, after kicking Badalia, would get money and a long-absent sense of satisfaction. There is much virtue in a creed or a law, but when all is prayed and suffered, drink is the only thing that will make clean all a man's deeds in his own eyes. Pity it is that the effects are not permanent.

Tom parted with his friends, bidding them tell Jenny that he was going to Gunnison Street, and would return to her arms no more. Because this was the devil's message, they remembered and severally delivered it, with drunken distinctness, in Jenny's ears. Then Tom took more drink till his drunkenness rolled back and stood off from him as a wave rolls back and stands off the wreck it will swamp. He reached the traffic-polished black asphalt of a side street and trod warily among the reflections of the shop-lamps that burned in gulfs of pitchy darkness, fathoms beneath his boot-heels. He was very sober indeed. Looking down his past, he beheld that he was justified of all his actions so entirely and perfectly that if Badalia had in his absence dared to lead a blameless life he would smash her for not having gone wrong.

Badalia at that moment was in her own room after the regular nightly skirmish with Lascar Loo's mother. To a reproof as stinging as a Gunnison Street tongue could make it, the old woman, detected for the hundredth time in the theft of the poor delicacies meant for the invalid, could only cackle and answer —

"D' you think Loo's never bilked in 'er life?
206

She's dyin' now — on'y she's so cunning long about it. Me! I'll live for twenty years yet."

Badalia shook her, more on principle than in any hope of curing her, and thrust her into the night, where she collapsed on the pavement and called upon the Devil to slay Badalia.

He came upon the word in the shape of a man with a very pale face who asked for her by name. Lascar Loo's mother remembered. It was Badalia's husband — and the return of a husband to Gunnison Street was generally followed by beatings.

" Where's my wife? " said Tom. " Where's my slut of a wife? "

" Up-stairs an' be —— to her," said the old woman, falling over on her side. " 'Ave you come back for 'er, Tom? "

" Yes. 'Oo's she took up while I've bin gone? "

" All the bloomin' curicks in the parish. She's that set up you wouldn't know 'er."

" 'Strewth she is! "

" Oh, yuss. More'n that, she's always round an' about with them sniffin' Sisters o' Charity an' the curick. More'n that, 'e gives 'er money — pounds an' pounds a week. 'Been keepin' her that way for months, 'e 'as. No wonder you wouldn't 'ave nothin' to do with 'er when you left. An' she keeps me outer the food-stuff they gets for me lyin' dyin' out 'ere like a dorg. She's been a blazin' bad un has Badalia since you lef'."

" Got the same room still, 'as she ? " said Tom, striding over Lascar Loo's mother, who was picking at the chinks between the pave-stones.

" Yes, but so fine you wouldn't know it."

Tom went up the stairs and the old lady chuckled. Tom was angry. Badalia would not be able to bump people for some time to come, or to interfere with the heaven-appointed distribution of custards.

Badalia, undressing to go to bed, heard feet on the stair that she knew well. Ere they stopped to kick at her door she had, in her own fashion, thought over very many things.

" Tom's back," she said to herself. " An' I'm glad . . . spite o' the curick an' everythink."

She opened the door, crying his name.

The man pushed her aside.

" I don't want none o' your kissin's an' slaverin's. I'm sick of 'em," said he.

" You ain't 'ad so many neither to make you sick these two years past."

" I've 'ad better. 'Got any money ? "

" On'y a little — orful little."

" That's a —— lie, and you know it."

" 'Tain't — and, oh, Tom, what's the use o' talkin' money the minute you come back ? Didn't you like Jenny ? I knowed you wouldn't."

" Shut your 'ead. Ain't you got enough to make a man drunk fair ? "

"You don't want bein' made more drunk any. You're drunk a'ready. You come to bed, Tom."

"To you?"

"Ay, to me. Ain't I nothin' — spite o' Jenny?"

She put out her arms as she spoke. But the drink held Tom fast.

"Not for me," said he, steadying himself against the wall. "Don't I know 'ow you've been goin' on while I was away, yah!"

"Arsk about!" said Badalia, indignantly, drawing herself together. "'Oo sez anythink ag'in' me 'ere?"

"'Oo sez? W'y, everybody. I ain't come back more'n a minute 'fore I finds you've been with the curick Gawd knows where. Wot curick was 'e?"

"The curick that's 'ere always," said Badalia, hastily. She was thinking of anything rather than the Reverend Eustace Hanna at that moment. Tom sat down gravely in the only chair in the room. Badalia continued her arrangements for going to bed.

"Pretty thing that," said Tom, "to tell your own lawful married 'usband — an' I guv five bob for the weddin'-ring. Curick that's 'ere always! Cool as brass you are. Ain't you got no shame? Ain't 'e under the bed now?"

"Tom, you're bleedin' drunk. I ain't done nothin' to be 'shamed of."

" You ! You don't know wot shame is. But I ain't come 'ere to mess with you. Give me wot you've got, an' then I'll dress you down an' go to Jenny."

" I ain't got nothin' 'cept some coppers an' a shillin' or so."

" Wot's that about the curick keepin' you on five poun' a week ? "

" 'Oo told you that ? "

" Lascar Loo's mother, lyin' on the pavemint outside, an' more honest than you'll ever be. Give me wot you've got ! "

Badalia passed over to a little shell pincush-ion on the mantelpiece, drew thence four shil-lings and threepence — the lawful earnings of her mangle — and held them out to the man who was rocking in his chair and surveying the room with wide-opened rolling eyes.

" That ain't five poun'," said he, drowsily.

" I ain't got no more. Take it an' go — if you won't stay."

Tom rose slowly, gripping the arms of the chair. " Wot about the curick's money that 'e guv you ? " said he. " Lascar Loo's mother told me. You give it over to me now, or I'll make you."

" Lascar Loo's mother don't know anything about it."

" She do, an' more than you want her to know."

" She don't. I've bumped the 'eart out of 'er,

and I can't give you the money. Anythin' else but that, Tom, an' everythin' else but that, Tom, I'll give willin' and true. 'Tain't my money. Won't the dollar be enough? That money's my trust. There's a book along of it too."

"Your trust? Wot are you doin' with any trust that your 'usband don't know of? You an' your trust! Take you that!"

Tom stepped towards her and delivered a blow of the clinched fist across the mouth. "Give me wot you've got," said he, in the thick abstracted voice of one talking in dreams.

"I won't," said Badalia, staggering to the washstand. With any other man than her husband she would have fought savagely as a wild cat; but Tom had been absent two years, and, perhaps, a little timely submission would win him back to her. None the less, the weekly trust was sacred.

The wave that had so long held back descended on Tom's brain. He caught Badalia by the throat and forced her to her knees. It seemed just to him in that hour to punish an erring wife for two years of wilful desertion; and the more, in that she had confessed her guilt by refusing to give up the wage of sin.

Lascar Loo's mother waited on the pavement without for the sounds of lamentation, but none came. Even if Tom had released her throat, Badalia would not have screamed.

"Give it up, you slut!" said Tom. "Is that 'ow you pay me back for all I've done?"

"I can't. 'Tain't my money. Gawd forgive you, Tom, for wot you're —" the voice ceased as the grip tightened, and Tom heaved Badalia against the bed. Her forehead struck the bed-post, and she sank, half kneeling on the floor. It was impossible for a self-respecting man to refrain from kicking her: so Tom kicked with the deadly intelligence born of whisky. The head drooped to the floor, and Tom kicked at that till the crisp tingle of hair striking through his nailed boot with the chill of cold water warned him that it might be as well to desist.

"Where's the curick's money, you kep' wo-man?" he whispered in the blood-stained ear. But there was no answer — only a rattling at the door, and the voice of Jenny Wabstow crying ferociously, "Come out o' that, Tom, an' come 'ome with me! An' you, Badalia, I'll tear your face off its bones!"

Tom's friends had delivered their message, and Jenny, after the first flood of passionate tears, rose up to follow Tom, and, if possible, to win him back. She was prepared even to endure an exemplary whacking for her performances in Hennessy's Rents. Lascar Loo's mother guided her to the chamber of horrors, and chuckled as she retired down the staircase. If Tom had not banged

the soul out of Badalia, there would at least be
a royal fight between that Badalia and Jenny.
And Lascar Loo's mother knew well that Hell
has no fury like a woman fighting above the life
that is quick in her.

Still there was no sound in the street. Jenny
swung back the unbolted door, to discover her
man stupidly regarding a heap by the bed. An
eminent murderer has remarked that if people did
not die so untidily most men, and all women,
would commit at least one murder in their lives.
Tom was reflecting on the present untidiness, and
the whisky was fighting with the clear current of
his thoughts.

"Don't make that noise," he said. "Come in
quick."

"My Gawd!" said Jenny, checking like a
startled wild beast. "Wot's all this 'ere? You
ain't —"

"Dunno. S'pose I done it."

"Done it! You done it a sight too well this
time."

"She was aggravatin'," said Tom, thickly, drop-
ping back into the chair. "That aggravatin' you'd
never believe. Livin' on the fat o' the land among
these aristocratic parsons an' all. Look at them
white curtings on the bed. *We* ain't got no white
curtings. What I want to know is —" The
voice died as Badalia's had died, but from a dif-

ferent cause. The whisky was tightening its grip after the accomplished deed, and Tom's eyes were beginning to close. Badalia on the floor breathed heavily.

"No, nor like to 'ave," said Jenny. "You've done for 'er this time. You go!"

"Not me. She won't hurt. Do 'er good. I'm goin' to sleep. Look at those there clean sheets! Ain't you comin' too?"

Jenny bent over Badalia, and there was intelligence in the battered woman's eyes — intelligence and much hate.

"I never told 'im to do such," Jenny whispered. "'Twas Tom's own doin' — none o' mine. Shall I get 'im took, dearie?"

The eyes told their own story. Tom, who was beginning to snore, must not be taken by the Law.

"Go," said Jenny. "Get out! Get out of 'ere."

"You — told — me — that — this afternoon," said the man, very sleepily. "Lemme go asleep."

"That wasn't nothing. You'd only 'it me. This time it's murder—murder—murder! Tom, you've killed 'er now." She shook the man from his rest, and understanding with cold terror filled his fuddled brain.

"I done it for your sake, Jenny," he whimpered feebly, trying to take her hand.

"You killed 'er for the money, same as you

would ha' killed me. Get out o' this. Lay 'er on the bed first, you brute!"

They lifted Badalia on to the bed and crept forth silently.

"I can't be took along o' you — and if you was took you'd say I made you do it, an' try to get me 'anged. Go away — anywhere outer 'ere," said Jenny, and she dragged him down the stairs.

"Goin' to look for the curick?" said a voice from the pavement. Lascar Loo's mother was still waiting patiently to hear Badalia squeal.

"Wot curick?" said Jenny, swiftly. There was a chance of salving her conscience yet in regard to the bundle up-stairs.

"'Anna — 63 Roomer Terrace — close 'ere," said the old woman. She had never been favourably regarded by the curate. Perhaps, since Badalia had not squealed, Tom preferred smashing the man to the woman. There was no accounting for tastes.

Jenny thrust her man before her till they reached the nearest main road. "Go away, now," she gasped. "Go off anywheres, but don't come back to me. I'll never go with you again; an', Tom — Tom, d' yer 'ear me? — clean your boots."

Vain counsel. The desperate thrust of disgust which she bestowed upon him sent him staggering face down into the kennel, where a policeman showed interest in his welfare.

"Took for a common drunk. Gawd send they don't look at 'is boots! 'Anna, 63 Roomer Terrace!" Jenny settled her hat and ran.

The excellent housekeeper of the Roomer Chambers still remembers how there arrived a young person, blue-lipped and gasping, who cried only: "Badalia, 17 Gunnison Street. Tell the curick to come at once — at once — at once!" and vanished into the night. This message was borne to the Reverend Eustace Hanna, then enjoying his beauty sleep. He saw there was urgency in the demand, and unhesitatingly knocked up Brother Victor across the landing. As a matter of etiquette, Rome and England divided their cases in the district according to the creeds of the sufferers; but Badalia was an institution, and not a case, and there was no district-relief etiquette to be considered. "Something has happened to Badalia," the curate said, "and it's your affair as well as mine. Dress and come along."

"I am ready," was the answer. "Is there any hint of what's wrong?"

"Nothing beyond a runaway knock and a call."

"Then it's a confinement or a murderous assault. Badalia wouldn't wake us up for anything less. I'm qualified for both, thank God."

The two men raced to Gunnison Street, for there were no cabs abroad, and under any circumstances a cab fare means two days' good firing for such as

216

are perishing with cold. Lascar Loo's mother had gone to bed, and the door was naturally on the latch. They found considerably more than they had expected in Badalia's room, and the Church of Rome acquitted itself nobly with bandages, while the Church of England could only pray to be delivered from the sin of envy. The Order of Little Ease, recognising that the soul is in most cases accessible through the body, take their measures and train their men accordingly.

"She'll do now," said Brother Victor, in a whisper. "It's internal bleeding, I fear, and a certain amount of injury to the brain. She has a husband, of course?"

"They all have, more's the pity."

"Yes, there's a domesticity about these injuries that shows their origin." He lowered his voice. "It's a perfectly hopeless business, you understand. Twelve hours at the longest."

Badalia's right hand began to beat on the counterpane, palm down.

"I think you are wrong," said the Church of England. "She is going."

"No, that's not picking at the counterpane," said the Church of Rome. "She wants to say something; you know her better than I."

The curate bent very low.

"Send for Miss Eva," said Badalia, with a cough.

" In the morning. She will come in the morning," said the curate, and Badalia was content. Only the Church of Rome, who knew something of the human heart, knitted his brows and said nothing. After all, the law of his order was plain. His duty was to watch till the dawn while the grey worn moon went down.

It was a little before her sinking that the Reverend Eustace Hanna said, " Had n't we better send for Sister Eva ? She seems to be going fast."

Brother Victor made no answer, but as early as decency allowed there came one to the door of the house of the Little Sisters of the Red Diamond and demanded Sister Eva, that she might soothe the pain of Badalia Herodsfoot. That man, saying very little, led her to Gunnison Street, No. 17, and into the room where Badalia lay. Then he stood on the landing, and bit the flesh of his fingers in agony, because he was a priest trained to know, and knew how the hearts of men and women beat back at the rebound, so that Love is born out of horror, and passion declares itself when the soul is quivering with pain.

Badalia, wise to the last, husbanded her strength till the coming of Sister Eva. It is generally maintained by the Little Sisters of the Red Diamond that she died in delirium, but since one Sister at least took a half of her dying advice, this seems uncharitable.

She tried to turn feebly on the bed, and the poor broken human machinery protested according to its nature.

Sister Eva started forward, thinking that she heard the dread forerunner of the death-rattle. Badalia lay still conscious, and spoke with startling distinctness, the irrepressible irreverence of the street-hawker, the girl who had danced on the winkle-barrow, twinkling in her one available eye.

"'Sounds jest like Mrs. Jessel, don't it? Before she's 'ad 'er lunch an' 'as been talkin' all the mornin' to 'er classes."

Neither Sister Eva nor the curate said anything. Brother Victor stood without the door, and the breath came harshly between his clinched teeth, for he was in pain.

"Put a cloth over my 'ead," said Badalia. "I've got it good, an' I don't want Miss Eva to see. I ain't pretty this time."

"Who was it?" said the curate.

"Man from outside. Never seed 'im no more'n Adam. Drunk, I s'pose. S' 'elp me Gawd, that's truth! Is Miss Eva 'ere? I can't see under the towel. I've got it good, Miss Eva. Excuse my not shakin' 'ands with you, but I'm not strong; an' it's fourpence for Mrs. Imeny's beef-tea, an' wot you can give 'er for baby-linnin'. Allus 'avin' kids, these people. I 'adn't oughter talk, for *my* 'usband 'e never come nigh me these two

years, or I'd 'a' bin as bad as the rest; but 'e never
come nigh me. . . . A man come an' 'it me over
the 'ead, an' 'e kicked me, Miss Eva; so it was
just the same 's if I had ha' had a 'usband, ain't it?
The book's in the drawer, Mister 'Anna, an' it's
all right, an' I never guv up a copper o' the trust
money — not a copper. You look under the chist
o' drawers — all wot isn't spent this week is there.
. . . An', Miss Eva, don't you wear that grey bonnick no more. I kep' you from the diptheery,
an' — an' I didn't want to keep you so, but the
curick said it 'ad to be done. I'd 'a' sooner ha'
took up with 'im than any one, only Tom he come,
an' then — you see, Miss Eva, Tom 'e never come
nigh me for two years, nor I 'aven't seen him yet.
S' 'elp me ——, I 'aven't. Do you 'ear? But you
two go along, and make a match of it. I've
wished otherways often, but o' course it was not
for the likes o' me. If Tom 'ad come back, which
'e never did, I'd ha' been like the rest — sixpence
for beef-tea for the baby, an' a shilling for layin'
out the baby. You've seen it in the books, Mister
'Anna. That's what it is; an' o' course you
couldn't never 'ave nothing to do with me. But
a woman she wishes as she looks, an' never you
'ave no doubt about 'im, Miss Eva. I've seen it
in 'is face time an' ag'in — time an' ag'in. . . .
Make it a four pound ten funeral — with a pall."

It was a seven pound fifteen shilling funeral,

and all Gunnison Street turned out to do it honour. All but two; for Lascar Loo's mother saw that a power had departed, and that her road lay clear to the custards. Therefore, when the carriages rattled off, the cat on the door-step heard the wail of the dying prostitute who could not die:

"Oh, mother, mother, won't you even let me lick the spoon!"

MY SUNDAY AT HOME

MY SUNDAY AT HOME

If the Red Slayer think he slays,
   Or if the slain think he is slain,
They know not well the subtle ways
   I keep and pass and turn again.

                                    Emerson.

It was the unreproducible slid *r*, as he said this was his "fy-ist" visit to England, that told me he was a New-Yorker from New York; and when, in the course of our long, lazy journey westward from Waterloo, he enlarged upon the beauties of his city, I, professing ignorance, said no word. He had, amazed and delighted at the man's civility, given the London porter a shilling for carrying his bag nearly fifty yards; he had thoroughly investigated the first-class lavatory compartment, which the London and Southwestern sometimes supply without extra charge; and now, half-awed, half-contemptuous, but wholly interested, he looked out upon the ordered English landscape wrapped in its Sunday peace, while I watched the wonder grow upon his face. Why were the cars so short and stilted? Why had every other freight-car a tarpaulin drawn over it? What wages would an engineer get now? Where was the swarming population of England he had read so much about? What was the rank of all those men on tricycles along the roads? When were we due at Plymouth?

I told him all I knew, and very much that I did not. He was going to Plymouth to assist in a consultation upon a fellow-countryman who had retired to a place called The Hoe — was that up-town or down-town? — to recover from nervous dyspepsia. Yes, he himself was a doctor by profession, and how any one in England could retain any nervous disorder passed his comprehension. Never had he dreamed of an atmosphere so soothing. Even the deep rumble of London traffic was monastical by comparison with some cities he could name; and the country — why, it was Paradise. A continuance of it, he confessed, would drive him mad; but for a few months it was the most sumptuous rest-cure in his knowledge.

"I'll come over every year after this," he said, in a burst of delight, as we ran between two ten-foot hedges of pink and white may. "It's seeing all the things I've ever read about. Of course it doesn't strike you that way. I presume you belong here? What a finished land it is! It's arrived. 'Must have been born this way. Now, where I used to live — Hello! what's up?"

MY SUNDAY AT HOME

The train stopped in a blaze of sunshine at Framlynghame Admiral, which is made up entirely of the name-board, two platforms, and an overhead bridge, without even the usual siding. I had never known the slowest of locals stop here before; but on Sunday all things are possible to the London and Southwestern. One could hear the drone of conversation along the carriages, and, scarcely less loud, the drone of the bumblebees in the wallflowers up the bank. My companion thrust his head through the window and sniffed luxuriously.

" Where are we now ? " said he.

" In Wiltshire," said I.

" Ah ! A man ought to be able to write novels with his left hand in a country like this. Well, well ! And so this is about Tess's country, ain't it ? I feel just as if I were in a book. Say, the conduc — the guard has something on his mind. What's he getting at ? "

The splendid badged and belted guard was striding up the platform at the regulation official pace, and in the regulation official voice was saying at each door :

" Has any gentleman here a bottle of medicine ? A gentleman has taken a bottle of poison (laudanum) by mistake."

Between each five paces he looked at an official telegram in his hand, refreshed his memory, and said his say. The dreamy look on my companion's face — he had gone far away with Tess — passed with the speed of a snap-shutter. After the manner of his countrymen, he had risen to the situation, jerked his bag down from the overhead rail, opened it, and I heard the click of bottles. "Find out where the man is," he said briefly. "I've got something here that will fix him — if he can swallow still."

Swiftly I fled up the line of carriages in the wake of the guard. There was clamour in a rear compartment — the voice of one bellowing to be let out, and the feet of one who kicked. With the tail of my eye I saw the New York doctor hastening thither, bearing in his hand a blue and brimming glass from the lavatory compartment. The guard I found scratching his head unofficially, by the engine, and murmuring: "Well, I put a bottle of medicine off at Andover — I'm sure I did."

"Better say it again, any'ow," said the driver. "Orders is orders. Say it again."

Once more the guard paced back, I, anxious to attract his attention, trotting at his heels.

"In a minute — in a minute, sir," he said, waving an arm capable of starting all the traffic on the London and Southwestern Railway at a wave. "Has any gentleman here got a bottle of medicine? A gentleman has taken a bottle of poison (laudanum) by mistake."

"Where's the man?" I gasped.

"Woking. 'Ere's my orders." He showed me the telegram, on which were the words to be said. "'E must have left 'is bottle in the train, an' took another by mistake. 'E's been wirin' from Woking awful, an', now I come to think of it, I'm nearly sure I put a bottle of medicine off at Andover."

"Then the man that took the poison isn't in the train?"

"Lord, no, sir. No one didn't take poison *that* way. 'E took it away with 'im, in 'is 'ands. 'E's wirin' from Wokin'. My orders was to ask everybody in the train, and I 'ave, an' we're four minutes late now. Are you comin' on, sir? No? Right be'ind!"

There is nothing, unless, perhaps, the English language, more terrible than the workings of an English railway line. An instant before it seemed as though we were going to spend all eternity at Framlynghame Admiral, and now I was watching the tail of the train disappear round the curve of the cutting.

But I was not alone. On the one bench of the down platform sat the largest navvy I have ever seen in my life, softened and made affable (for he smiled generously) with liquor. In his huge hands he nursed an empty tumbler marked "L. S. W. R."—marked also, internally, with streaks of blue-grey sediment. Before him, a hand on his shoulder, stood the doctor, and as I came within ear-shot, this is what I heard him say : "Just you hold on to your patience for a minute or two longer, and you'll be as right as ever you were in your life. *I'll* stay with you till you're better."

"Lord! I'm comfortable enough," said the navvy. "'Never felt better in my life."

Turning to me, the doctor lowered his voice. "He might have died while that fool conduct — guard was saying his piece. I've fixed him, though. The stuff's due in about five minutes, but there's a heap *to* him. I don't see how we can make him take exercise."

For the moment I felt as though seven pounds of crushed ice had been neatly applied in the form of a compress to my lower stomach.

"How — how did you manage it?" I gasped.

"I asked him if he'd have a drink. He was knocking spots out of the car — strength of his constitution, I suppose. He said he'd go 'most anywhere for a drink, so I lured on to the platform, and loaded him up. 'Cold-blooded people, you Britishers are. That train's gone, and no one seemed to care a cent."

"We've missed it," I said.

He looked at me curiously.

"We'll get another before sundown, if that's

your only trouble. Say, porter, when's the next train down?"

"Seven forty-five," said the one porter, and passed out through the wicket-gate into the landscape. It was then three-twenty of a hot and sleepy afternoon. The station was absolutely deserted. The navvy had closed his eyes, and now nodded.

"That's bad," said the doctor. "The man, I mean, not the train. We must make him walk somehow — walk up and down."

Swiftly as might be, I explained the delicacy of the situation, and the doctor from New York turned a full bronze-green. Then he swore comprehensively at the entire fabric of our glorious Constitution, cursing the English language, root, branch, and paradigm, through its most obscure derivatives. His coat and bag lay on the bench next to the sleeper. Thither he edged cautiously, and I saw treachery in his eye.

What devil of delay possessed him to slip on his spring overcoat, I cannot tell. They say a slight noise rouses a sleeper more surely than a heavy one, and scarcely had the doctor settled himself in his sleeves than the giant waked and seized that silk-faced collar in a hot right hand. There was rage in his face — rage and the realisation of new emotions.

"I'm — I'm not so comfortable as I were," he

said from the deeps of his interior. "You'll wait along o' me, *you* will." He breathed heavily through shut lips.

Now, if there was one thing more than another upon which the doctor had dwelt in his conversation with me, it was upon the essential law-abidingness, not to say gentleness, of his much-misrepresented country. And yet (truly, it may have been no more than a button that irked him) I saw his hand travel backwards to his right hip, clutch at something, and come away empty.

"He won't kill you," I said. "He'll probably sue you in court, if I know my own people. Better give him some money from time to time."

"If he keeps quiet till the stuff gets in its work," the doctor answered, "I'm all right. If he doesn't . . . my name is Emory — Julian B. Emory — 193 'Steenth Street, corner of Madison and —"

"I feel worse than I've ever felt," said the navvy, with suddenness. "What — did — you — give — me — the — drink — for?"

The matter seemed to be so purely personal that I withdrew to a strategic position on the overhead bridge, and, abiding in the exact centre, looked on from afar.

I could see the white road that ran across the shoulder of Salisbury Plain, unshaded for mile after mile, and a dot in the middle distance, the back of the one porter returning to Framlynghame Admiral, if such a place existed, till seven forty-five. The bell of a church invisible clanked softly. There was a rustle in the horse-chestnuts to the left of the line, and the sound of sheep cropping close.

The peace of Nirvana lay upon the land, and, brooding in it, my elbow on the warm iron girder of the foot-bridge (it is a forty-shilling fine to cross by any other means), I perceived, as never before, how the consequences of our acts run eternal through time and through space. If we impinge never so slightly upon the life of a fellow-mortal, the touch of our personality, like the ripple of a stone cast into a pond, widens and widens in unending circles across the æons, till the far-off Gods themselves cannot say where action ceases. Also, it was I who had silently set before the doctor the tumbler of the first-class lavatory compartment now speeding Plymouthward. Yet I was, in spirit at least, a million leagues removed from that unhappy man of another nationality, who had chosen to thrust an inexpert finger into the workings of an alien life. The machinery was dragging him up and down the sunlit platform. The two men seemed to be learning polka-mazurkas together, and the burden of their song, borne by one deep voice, was: " What did you give me the drink for ? "

I saw the flash of silver in the doctor's hand. The navvy took it and pocketed it with his left; but never for an instant did his strong right leave the doctor's coat-collar, and as the crisis approached, louder and louder rose his bull-like roar: " What did you give me the drink for ? "

They drifted under the great twelve-inch pinned timbers of the foot-bridge towards the bench, and, I gathered, the time was very near at hand. The stuff was getting in its work. Blue, white, and blue again, rolled over the navvy's face in waves, till all settled to one rich clay-bank yellow and — that fell which fell.

I thought of the blowing up of Hell Gate; of the geysers in the Yellowstone Park; of Jonah and his whale : but the lively original, as I watched it foreshortened from above, exceeded all these things. He staggered to the bench, the heavy wooden seat cramped with iron cramps into the enduring stone, and clung there with his left hand. It quivered and shook, as a breakwater-pile quivers to the rush of landward-racing seas; nor was there lacking, when he caught his breath, the " scream of a maddened beach dragged down by the tide." His right hand was upon the doctor's collar, so that the two shook to one paroxysm, pendulums vibrating together, while I, apart, shook with them.

It was colossal — immense; but of certain manifestations the English language stops short. French only, the caryatid French of Victor Hugo, would have described it; so I mourned while I laughed, hastily shuffling and discarding inadequate adjectives. The vehemence of the shock spent itself, and the sufferer half fell, half knelt, across the bench. He was calling now upon God and his wife, huskily, as the wounded bull calls upon the unscathed herd to stay. Curiously enough, he used no bad language : that had gone from him with the rest. The doctor exhibited gold. It was taken and retained. So, too, was the grip on the coat-collar.

"If I could stand," boomed the giant, despairingly, "I'd smash you — you an' your drinks. I'm dyin' — dyin' — dyin' ! "

"That's what you think," said the doctor. "You'll find it will do you a lot of good"; and, making a virtue of a somewhat imperative necessity, he added : "I'll stay by you. If you'd let go of me a minute I'd give you something that would settle you."

"You've settled me now, you damned anarchist. Takin' the bread out of the mouth of an English workin'-man! But I'll keep 'old of you till I'm well or dead. I never did you no 'arm. S'pose I *were* a little full. They pumped me out once at Guy's with a stummick-pump. I could see *that*, but I can't see this 'ere, an' it's killin' of me by slow degrees."

"You'll be all right in half-an-hour. What do you suppose I'd want to kill you for?" said the doctor, who came of a logical breed.

"'Ow do *I* know? Tell 'em in court. You'll get seven years for this, you body-snatcher. That's what you are — a bloomin' body-snatcher. There's justice, I tell you, in England; and my Union 'll prosecute, too. We don't stand no tricks with people's insides 'ere. They give a woman ten years for a sight less than this. An' you'll 'ave to pay 'undreds an' 'undreds o' pounds, besides a pension to the missus. *You'll* see, you physickin' furriner. Where's your licence to do such? *You'll* catch it, I tell you!"

Then I observed what I have frequently observed before, that a man who is but reasonably afraid of an altercation with an alien has a most poignant dread of the operations of foreign law. The doctor's voice was flute-like in its exquisite politeness, as he answered:

"But I've given you a very great deal of money — fif — three pounds, I think."

"An' what's three pound for poisonin' the likes o' *me?* They told me at Guy's I'd fetch twenty — cold — on the slates. Ouh! It's comin' again."

A second time he was cut down by the foot, as it were, and the straining bench rocked to and fro as I averted my eyes.

MY SUNDAY AT HOME

It was the very point of perfection in the heart of an English May-day. The unseen tides of the air had turned, and all nature was setting its face with the shadows of the horse-chestnuts towards the peace of the coming night. But there were hours yet, I knew — long, long hours of the eternal English twilight — to the ending of the day. I was well content to be alive — to abandon myself to the drift of Time and Fate; to absorb great peace through my skin, and to love my country with the devotion that three thousand miles of intervening sea bring to fullest flower. And what a garden of Eden it was, this fatted, clipped, and washen land! A man could camp in any open field with more sense of home and security than the stateliest buildings of foreign cities could afford. And the joy was that it was all mine alienably — groomed hedgerow, spotless road, decent grey-stone cottage, serried spinney, tasselled copse, apple-bellied hawthorn, and well-grown tree. A light puff of wind — it scattered flakes of may over the gleaming rails — gave me a faint whiff as it might have been of fresh cocoanut, and I knew that the golden gorse was in bloom somewhere out of sight. Linnæus had thanked God on his bended knees when he first saw a field of it; and, by the way, the navvy was on his knees, too. But he was by no means praying. He was purely disgustful.

The doctor was compelled to bend over him, his face towards the back of the seat, and from what I had seen I supposed the navvy was now dead. If that were the case it would be time for me to go; but I knew that so long as a man trusts himself to the current of Circumstance, reaching out for and rejecting nothing that comes his way, no harm can overtake him. It is the contriver, the schemer, who is caught by the Law, and never the philosopher. I knew that when the play was played, Destiny herself would move me on from the corpse; and I felt very sorry for the doctor.

In the far distance, presumably upon the road that led to Framlynghame Admiral, there appeared a vehicle and a horse — the one ancient fly that almost every village can produce at need. This thing was advancing, unpaid by me, towards the station; would have to pass along the deep-cut lane, below the railway-bridge, and come out on the doctor's side. I was in the centre of things, so all sides were alike to me. Here, then, was my machine from the machine. When it arrived, something would happen, or something else. For the rest, I owned my deeply interested soul.

The doctor, by the seat, turned so far as his cramped position allowed, his head over his left shoulder, and laid his right hand upon his lips.

I threw back my hat and elevated my eyebrows in the form of a question. The doctor shut his eyes and nodded his head slowly twice or thrice, beckoning me to come. I descended cautiously, and it was as the signs had told. The navvy was asleep, empty to the lowest notch; yet his hand clutched still the doctor's collar, and at the lightest movement (the doctor was really very cramped) tightened mechanically, as the hand of a sick woman tightens on that of the watcher. He had dropped, squatting almost upon his heels, and, falling lower, had dragged the doctor over to the left.

The doctor thrust his right hand, which was free, into his pocket, drew forth some keys, and shook his head. The navvy gurgled in his sleep. Silently I dived into my pocket, took out one sovereign, and held it up between finger and thumb. Again the doctor shook his head. Money was not what was lacking to his peace. His bag had fallen from the seat to the ground. He looked towards it, and opened his mouth — O-shape. The catch was not a difficult one, and when I had mastered it, the doctor's right forefinger was sawing the air. With an immense caution, I extracted from the bag such a knife as they use for cutting collops off legs. The doctor frowned, and with his first and second fingers imitated the action of scissors. Again I searched, and found a most dia-

bolical pair of cock-nosed shears, capable of van-
dyking the interiors of elephants. The doctor
then slowly lowered his left shoulder till the
navvy's right wrist was supported by the bench,
pausing a moment as the spent volcano rumbled
anew. Lower and lower the doctor sank, kneeling now by the navvy's side, till his head was on
a level with, and just in front of, the great hairy
fist, and — there was no tension on the coat-collar.
Then light dawned on me.

Beginning a little to the right of the spinal column, I cut a huge demilune out of his new spring
overcoat, bringing it round as far under his left
side (which was the right side of the navvy) as I
dared. Passing thence swiftly to the back of the
seat, and reaching between the splines, I sawed
through the silk-faced front on the left-hand side
of the coat till the two cuts joined.

Cautiously as the box-turtle of his native heath,
the doctor drew away sideways and to the right,
with the air of a frustrated burglar coming out
from under a bed, and stood up free, one black
diagonal shoulder projecting through the grey of
his ruined overcoat. I returned the scissors to the
bag, snapped the catch, and held all out to him as
the wheels of the fly rang hollow under the railway arch.

It came at a footpace past the wicket-gate of
the station, and the doctor stopped it with a whis-

per. It was going some five miles across country to bring home from church some one — I could not catch the name — because his own carriage-horses were lame. Its destination happened to be the one place in all the world that the doctor was most burningly anxious to visit, and he promised the driver untold gold to drive to some ancient flame of his — Helen Blazes, she was called.

"Aren't you coming, too?" he said, bundling his overcoat into his bag.

Now the fly had been so obviously sent to the doctor, and to no one else, that I had no concern with it. Our roads, I saw, divided, and there was, further, a need upon me to laugh.

"I shall stay here," I said. "It's a very pretty country."

"My God!" he murmured, as softly as he shut the door, and I felt that it was a prayer.

Then he went out of my life, and I shaped my course for the railway-bridge. It was necessary to pass by the bench once more, but the wicket was between us. The departure of the fly had waked the navvy. He crawled on to the seat, and with malignant eyes watched the driver flog down the road.

"The man inside o' that," he called, "'as poisoned me. 'E's a body-snatcher. 'E's comin' back again when I'm cold. 'Ere's my evidence!"

He waved his share of the overcoat, and I went

my way, because I was hungry. Framlynghame Admiral village is a good two miles from the station, and I waked the holy calm of the evening every step of that way with shouts and yells, casting myself down in the flank of the good green hedge when I was too weak to stand. There was an inn,— a blessed inn with a thatched roof, and peonies in the garden,— and I ordered myself an upper chamber in which the Foresters held their courts, for the laughter was not all out of me. A bewildered woman brought me ham and eggs, and I leaned out of the mullioned window, and laughed between mouthfuls. I sat long above the beer and the perfect smoke that followed, till the lights changed in the quiet street, and I began to think of the seven forty-five down, and all that world of the "Arabian Nights" I had quitted.

Descending, I passed a giant in moleskins who filled the low-ceiled tap-room. Many empty plates stood before him, and beyond them a fringe of the Framlynghame Admiralty, to whom he was unfolding a wondrous tale of anarchy, of bodysnatching, of bribery, and the Valley of the Shadow from the which he was but newly risen. And as he talked he ate, and as he ate he drank, for there was much room in him; and anon he paid royally, speaking of Justice and the Law, before whom all Englishmen are equal, and all foreigners and anarchists vermin and slime.

On my way to the station, he passed me with great strides, his head high among the low-flying bats, his feet firm on the packed road-metal, his fists clinched, and his breath coming sharply. There was a beautiful smell in the air — the smell of white dust, bruised nettles, and smoke, that brings tears to the throat of a man who sees his country but seldom — a smell like the echoes of the lost talk of lovers; the infinitely suggestive odour of an immemorial civilisation. It was a perfect walk; and, lingering on every step, I came to the station just as the one porter lighted the last of a truck-load of lamps, and set them back in the lamp-room, while he dealt tickets to four or five of the population who, not contented with their own peace, thought fit to travel. It was no ticket that the navvy seemed to need. He was sitting on a bench, wrathfully grinding a tumbler into fragments with his heel. I abode in obscurity at the end of the platform, interested as ever, thank Heaven, in my surroundings. There was a jar of wheels on the road. The navvy rose as they approached, strode through the wicket, and laid a hand upon a horse's bridle that brought the beast up on his hireling hind legs. It was the providential fly coming back, and for a moment I wondered whether the doctor had been mad enough to revisit his practice.

"Get away; you're drunk," said the driver.

"I'm not," said the navvy. "I've been waitin' 'ere hours and hours. Come out, you beggar inside there!"

"Go on, driver," said a voice I did not know —a crisp, clear, English voice.

"All right," said the navvy. "You wouldn't 'ear me when I was polite. *Now* will you come?"

There was a chasm in the side of the fly, for he had wrenched the door bodily off its hinges, and was feeling within purposefully. A well-booted leg rewarded him, and there came out, not with delight, hopping on one foot, a round and grey-haired Englishman, from whose armpits dropped hymn-books, but from his mouth an altogether different service of song.

"Come on, you bloomin' body-snatcher! You thought I was dead, did you?" roared the navvy. And the respectable gentleman came accordingly, inarticulate with rage.

"'Ere's a man murderin' the Squire," the driver shouted, and fell from his box upon the navvy's neck.

To do them justice, the people of Framlynghame Admiral, so many as were on the platform, rallied to the call in the best spirit of feudalism. It was the one porter who beat the navvy on the nose with a ticket-punch, but it was the three third-class tickets who attached themselves to his legs and freed the captive.

"Send for a constable! lock him up!" said that man, adjusting his collar; and unitedly they cast him into the lamp-room, and turned the key, while the driver mourned over the wrecked fly.

Till then the navvy, whose only desire was justice, had kept his temper nobly. Then he went Berserk before our amazed eyes. The door of the lamp-room was generously constructed, and would not give an inch, but the window he tore from its fastenings and hurled outwards. The one porter counted the damage in a loud voice, and the others, arming themselves with agricultural implements from the station garden, kept up a ceaseless winnowing before the window, themselves backed close to the wall, and bade the prisoner think of the jail. He answered little to the point, so far as they could understand; but seeing that his exit was impeded, he took a lamp and hurled it through the wrecked sash. It fell on the metals and went out. With inconceivable velocity, the others, fifteen in all, followed, looking like rockets in the gloom, and with the last (he could have had no plan) the Berserk rage left him as the doctor's deadly brewage waked up, under the stimulus of violent exercise and a very full meal, to one last cataclysmal exhibition, and — we heard the whistle of the seven forty-five down.

They were all acutely interested in as much of the wreck as they could see, for the station smelt to Heaven of oil, and the engine skittered over broken glass like a terrier in a cucumber-frame. The guard had to hear of it, and the Squire had his version of the brutal assault, and heads were out all along the carriages as I found me a seat.

"What is the row?" said a young man, as I entered. "'Man drunk?"

"Well, the symptoms, so far as my observation has gone, more resemble those of Asiatic cholera than anything else," I answered, slowly and judicially, that every word might carry weight in the appointed scheme of things. Up till then, you will observe, I had taken no part in that war.

He was an Englishman, but he collected his belongings as swiftly as had the American, ages before, and leaped upon the platform, crying: "Can I be of any service? I'm a doctor."

From the lamp-room I heard a wearied voice wailing: "Another bloomin' doctor!"

And the seven forty-five carried me on, a step nearer to Eternity, by the road that is worn and seamed and channelled with the passions, and weaknesses, and warring interests of man who is immortal and master of his fate.

THE BRUSHWOOD BOY

THE BRUSHWOOD BOY

Girls and boys, come out to play :
The moon is shining as bright as day!
Leave your supper and leave your sleep,
And come with your playfellows out in the street!
Up the ladder and down the wall —

A CHILD of three sat up in his crib and screamed at the top of his voice, his fists clinched and his eyes full of terror. At first no one heard, for his nursery was in the west wing, and the nurse was talking to a gardener among the laurels. Then the housekeeper passed that way, and hurried to soothe him. He was her special pet, and she disapproved of the nurse.

"What was it, then? What was it, then? There's nothing to frighten him, Georgie dear."

"It was — it was a policeman! He was on the Down — I saw him! He came in. Jane *said* he would."

"Policemen don't come into houses, dearie. Turn over, and take my hand."

"I saw him — on the Down. He came here. Where is your hand, Harper?"

The housekeeper waited till the sobs changed to the regular breathing of sleep before she stole out.

"Jane, what nonsense have you been telling Master Georgie about policemen?"

"I haven't told him anything."

"You have. He's been dreaming about them."

"We met Tisdall on Dowhead when we were in the donkey-cart this morning. P'r'aps that's what put it into his head."

"Oh! Now you aren't going to frighten the child into fits with your silly tales, and the master know nothing about it. If ever I catch you again," etc.

* * * * * * * * * *

A child of six was telling himself stories as he lay in bed. It was a new power, and he kept it a secret. A month before it had occurred to him to carry on a nursery tale left unfinished by his mother, and he was delighted to find the tale as it came out of his own head just as surprising as though he were listening to it "all new from the beginning." There was a prince in that tale, and he killed dragons, but only for one night. Ever afterwards Georgie dubbed himself prince, pasha, giant-killer, and all the rest (you see, he could not tell any one, for fear of being laughed at), and his tales faded gradually into dreamland, where adventures were so many that he could not recall

THE BRUSHWOOD BOY

"and the races and adventures began"

the half of them. They all began in the same way, or, as Georgie explained to the shadows of the night-light, there was "the same starting-off place"—a pile of brushwood stacked somewhere near a beach; and round this pile Georgie found himself running races with little boys and girls. These ended, ships ran high up the dry land and opened into cardboard boxes; or gilt-and-green iron railings that surrounded beautiful gardens turned all soft and could be walked through and overthrown so long as he remembered it was only a dream. He could never hold that knowledge more than a few seconds ere things became real, and instead of pushing down houses full of grown-up people (a just revenge), he sat miserably upon gigantic door-steps trying to sing the multiplication-table up to four times six.

The princess of his tales was a person of wonderful beauty (she came from the old illustrated edition of Grimm, now out of print), and as she always applauded Georgie's valour among the dragons and buffaloes, he gave her the two finest names he had ever heard in his life—Annie and Louise, pronounced "Annie*an*louise." When the dreams swamped the stories, she would change into one of the little girls round the brushwood-pile, still keeping her title and crown. She saw Georgie drown once in a dream-sea by the beach (it was the day after he had been taken to bathe

in a real sea by his nurse); and he said as he sank :
"Poor Annie*an*louise! She'll be sorry for me
now!" But "Annie*an*louise," walking slowly on
the beach, called, "'Ha! ha!' said the duck, laughing," which to a waking mind might not seem to
bear on the situation. It consoled Georgie at
once, and must have been some kind of spell, for
it raised the bottom of the deep, and he waded
out with a twelve-inch flower-pot on each foot.
As he was strictly forbidden to meddle with
flower-pots in real life, he felt triumphantly wicked.

* * * * * * * * * *

The movements of the grown-ups, whom
Georgie tolerated, but did not pretend to understand, removed his world, when he was seven
years old, to a place called "Oxford-on-a-visit."
Here were huge buildings surrounded by vast
prairies, with streets of infinite length, and, above
all, something called the "buttery," which Georgie
was dying to see, because he knew it must be
greasy, and therefore delightful. He perceived
how correct were his judgments when his nurse
led him through a stone arch into the presence of
an enormously fat man, who asked him if he would
like some bread and cheese. Georgie was used to
eat all round the clock, so he took what "buttery"
gave him, and would have taken some brown
liquid called "audit-ale" but that his nurse led
him away to an afternoon performance of a thing

called "Pepper's Ghost." This was intensely thrilling. People's heads came off and flew all over the stage, and skeletons danced bone by bone, while Mr. Pepper himself, beyond question a man of the worst, waved his arms and flapped a long gown, and in a deep bass voice (Georgie had never heard a man sing before) told of his sorrows unspeakable. Some grown-up or other tried to explain that the illusion was made with mirrors, and that there was no need to be frightened. Georgie did not know what illusions were, but he did know that a mirror was the looking-glass with the ivory handle on his mother's dressing-table. Therefore the "grown-up" was "just saying things" after the distressing custom of "grown-ups," and Georgie cast about for amusement between scenes. Next to him sat a little girl dressed all in black, her hair combed off her forehead exactly like the girl in the book called "Alice in Wonderland," which had been given him on his last birthday. The little girl looked at Georgie, and Georgie looked at her. There seemed to be no need of any further introduction.

"I've got a cut on my thumb," said he. It was the first work of his first real knife, a savage triangular hack, and he esteemed it a most valuable possession.

"I'm tho thorry!" she lisped. "Let me look — pleathe."

"There's a di-ack-lum plaster on, but it's all raw under," Georgie answered, complying.

"Dothent it hurt?" — her grey eyes were full of pity and interest.

"Awf'ly. Perhaps it will give me lockjaw."

"It lookth very horrid. I'm *tho* thorry!" She put a forefinger to his hand, and held her head sidewise for a better view.

Here the nurse turned, and shook him severely. "You mustn't talk to strange little girls, Master Georgie."

"She isn't strange. She's very nice. I like her, an' I've showed her my new cut."

"The idea! You change places with me."

She moved him over, and shut out the little girl from his view, while the grown-up behind renewed the futile explanations.

"I am *not* afraid, truly," said the boy, wriggling in despair; "but why don't you go to sleep in the afternoons, same as Provost of Oriel?"

Georgie had been introduced to a grown-up of that name, who slept in his presence without apology. Georgie understood that he was the most important grown-up in Oxford; hence he strove to gild his rebuke with flatteries. This grown-up did not seem to like it, but he collapsed, and Georgie lay back in his seat, silent and enraptured. Mr. Pepper was singing again, and the deep, ringing voice, the red fire, and the misty, waving gown all seemed to be mixed up with the little girl who had been so kind about his cut. When the performance was ended she nodded to Georgie, and Georgie nodded in return. He spoke no more than was necessary till bedtime, but meditated on new colours and sounds and lights and music and things as far as he understood them; the deep-mouthed agony of Mr. Pepper mingling with the little girl's lisp. That night he made a new tale, from which he shamelessly removed the Rapun-zel-Rapunzel-let-down-your-hair princess, gold crown, Grimm edition, and all, and put a new Annie*an*louise in her place. So it was perfectly right and natural that when he came to the brush-wood-pile he should find her waiting for him, her hair combed off her forehead more like Alice in Wonderland than ever, and the races and adventures began.

* * * * * * * * *

Ten years at an English public school do not encourage dreaming. Georgie won his growth and chest measurement, and a few other things which did not appear in the bills, under a system of cricket, football, and paper-chases, from four to five days a week, which provided for three lawful cuts of a ground-ash if any boy absented himself from these entertainments. He became a rumple-collared, dusty-hatted fag of the Lower Third, and a light half-back at Little Side football; was pushed and prodded through the slack back-waters of the Lower Fourth, where the raffle of a school generally accumulates; won his "second-fifteen" cap at football, enjoyed the dignity of a study with two companions in it, and began to look forward to office as a sub-prefect. At last he blossomed into full glory as head of the school, ex-officio captain of the games; head of his house, where he and his lieutenants preserved discipline and decency among seventy boys from twelve to seventeen; general arbiter in the quarrels that spring up among the touchy Sixth — and intimate friend and ally of the Head himself. When he stepped forth in the black jersey, white knickers, and black stockings of the First Fifteen, the new match-ball under his arm, and his old and frayed cap at the back of his head, the small fry of the lower forms stood apart and worshipped, and the "new caps" of the team talked to him ostentatiously, that the world might see. And so, in summer, when he came back to the pavilion after a slow but eminently safe game, it mattered not whether he had made nothing or, as once happened, a hundred and three, the school shouted just the same, and women-folk who had come to look at the match looked at Cottar — Cottar, *major;* "that's Cottar!" Above all, he was responsible for that thing called the tone of the school, and few realise with what passionate devotion a certain type of boy throws himself into this work. Home was a far-away country, full of ponies and fishing and shooting, and men-visitors who interfered with one's plans; but school was the real world, where things of vital importance happened, and crises arose that must be dealt with promptly and quietly. Not for nothing was it written, " Let the Consuls look to it that the Republic takes no harm," and Georgie was glad to be back in authority when the holidays ended. Behind him, but not too near, was the wise and temperate Head, now suggesting the wisdom of the serpent, now counselling the mildness of the dove; leading him on to see, more by half-hints than by any direct word, how boys and men are all of a piece, and how he who can handle the one will assuredly in time control the other.

For the rest, the school was not encouraged to dwell on its emotions, but rather to keep in hard condition, to avoid false quantities, and to enter the army direct, without the help of the expensive London crammer, under whose roof young blood learns too much. Cottar, *major*, went the way of hundreds before him. The Head gave him six months' final polish, taught him what kind of answers best please a certain kind of examiners, and handed him over to the properly constituted authorities, who passed him into Sandhurst. Here he had sense enough to see that he was in the

Lower Third once more, and behaved with respect towards his seniors, till they in turn respected him, and he was promoted to the rank of corporal, and sat in authority over mixed peoples with all the vices of men and boys combined. His reward was another string of athletic cups, a good-conduct sword, and, at last, Her Majesty's commission as a subaltern in a first-class line regiment. He did not know that he bore with him from school and college a character worth much fine gold, but was pleased to find his mess so kindly. He had plenty of money of his own; his training had set the public-school mask upon his face, and had taught him how many were the "things no fellow can do." By virtue of the same training he kept his pores open and his mouth shut.

The regular working of the Empire shifted his world to India, where he tasted utter loneliness in subaltern's quarters — one room and one bullock-trunk — and, with his mess, learned the new life from the beginning. But there were horses in the land — ponies at reasonable price; there was polo for such as could afford it; there were the disreputable remnants of a pack of hounds; and Cottar worried his way along without too much despair. It dawned on him that a regiment in India was nearer the chance of active service than he had conceived, and that a man might as well study his profession. A major of the new school backed this idea with enthusiasm, and he and Cottar accumulated a library of military works, and read and argued and disputed far into the nights. But the adjutant said the old thing: "Get to know your men, young un, and they'll follow you anywhere. That's all you want — know your men." Cottar thought he knew them fairly well at cricket and the regimental sports, but he never realised the true inwardness of them till he was sent off with a detachment of twenty to sit down in a mud fort near a rushing river which was spanned by a bridge of boats. When the floods came they went forth and hunted strayed pontoons along the banks. Otherwise there was nothing to do, and the men got drunk, gambled, and quarrelled. They were a sickly crew, for a junior subaltern is by custom saddled with the worst men. Cottar endured their rioting as long as he could, and then sent down-country for a dozen pairs of boxing-gloves.

"I wouldn't blame you for fightin'," said he, "if you only knew how to use your hands; but you don't. Take these things, and I'll show you." The men appreciated his efforts. Now, instead of blaspheming and swearing at a comrade, and threatening to shoot him, they could take him apart, and soothe themselves to exhaustion. As one explained whom Cottar found with a shut eye and a diamond-shaped mouth spitting blood through an embrasure: "We tried it with the gloves, sir, for twenty minutes, and *that* done us no good, sir. Then we took off the gloves and tried it that way for another twenty minutes, same as you showed us, sir, an' that done us a world o' good. 'Twasn't fightin', sir; there was a bet on."

Cottar dared not laugh, but he invited his men to other sports, such as racing across country in shirt and trousers after a trail of torn paper, and to single-stick in the evenings, till the native population, who had a lust for sport in every form, wished to know whether the white men understood wrestling. They sent in an ambassador, who took the soldiers by the neck and threw them about the dust; and the entire command were all for this new game. They spent money on learning new falls and holds, which was better than buying other doubtful commodities; and the peasantry grinned five deep round the tournaments.

That detachment, who had gone up in bullock-carts, returned to headquarters at an average rate of thirty miles a day, fair heel-and-toe; no sick, no prisoners, and no court martials pending. They scattered themselves among their friends, singing the praises of their lieutenant and looking for causes of offence.

"How did you do it, young un?" the adjutant asked.

"Oh, I sweated the beef off 'em, and then I

sweated some muscle on to 'em. It was rather a lark."

"If that's your way of lookin' at it, we can give you all the larks you want. Young Davies isn't feelin' quite fit, and he's next for detachment duty. 'Care to go for him?"

"'Sure he wouldn't mind? I don't want to shove myself forward, you know."

"You needn't bother on Davies's account. We'll give you the sweepin's of the corps, and you can see what you can make of 'em."

"All right," said Cottar. "It's better fun than loafin' about cantonments."

"Rummy thing," said the adjutant, after Cottar had returned to his wilderness with twenty other devils worse than the first. "If Cottar only knew it, half the women in the station would give their eyes — confound 'em! — to have the young un in tow."

"That accounts for Mrs. Elery sayin' I was workin' my nice new boy too hard," said a wing commander.

"Oh, yes; and 'Why doesn't he come to the band-stand in the evenings?' and 'Can't I get him to make up a four at tennis with the Hammon girls?'" the adjutant snorted. "Look at young Davies makin' an ass of himself over mutton-dressed-as-lamb old enough to be his mother!"

"No one can accuse young Cottar of runnin'

after women, white *or* black," the major replied
thoughtfully. "But, then, that's the kind that
generally goes the worst mucker in the end."

"Not Cottar. I've only run across one of his
muster before — a fellow called Ingles, in South
Africa. He was just the same hard-trained, ath-
letic-sports build of animal. Always kept himself in the pink of condition. Didn't do him
much good, though. 'Shot at Wesselstroom the
week before Majuba. Wonder how the young
un will lick his detachment into shape."

Cottar turned up six weeks later, on foot,
with his pupils. He never told his experiences,
but the men spoke enthusiastically, and fragments
of it leaked back to the colonel through sergeants,
bâtmen, and the like.

There was great jealousy between the first and
second detachments, but the men united in adoring Cottar, and their way of showing it was by
sparing him all the trouble that men know how
to make for an unloved officer. He sought pop-
ularity as little as he had sought it at school, and
therefore it came to him. He favoured no one —
not even when the company sloven pulled the
company cricket-match out of the fire with an
unexpected forty-three at the last moment. There
was very little getting round him, for he seemed
to know by instinct exactly when and where to
head off a malingerer; but he did not forget that

the difference between a dazed and sulky junior of the upper school and a bewildered, browbeaten lump of a private fresh from the depot was very small indeed. The sergeants, seeing these things, told him secrets generally hid from young officers. His words were quoted as barrack authority on bets in canteen and at tea; and the veriest shrew of the corps, bursting with charges against other women who had used the cooking-ranges out of turn, forbore to speak when Cottar, as the regulations ordained, asked of a morning if there were " any complaints."

"I'm full o' complaints," said Mrs. Corporal Morrison, " an' I'd kill O'Halloran's fat sow of a wife any day, but ye know how it is. 'E puts 'is head just inside the door, an' looks down 'is blessed nose so bashful, an' 'e whispers, ' Any complaints ? ' Ye can't complain after that. *I* want to kiss him. Some day I think I will. Heigh-ho! she'll be a lucky woman that gets Young Innocence. See 'im now, girls. Do ye blame me ? "

Cottar was cantering across to polo, and he looked a very satisfactory figure of a man as he gave easily to the first excited bucks of his pony, and slipped over a low mud wall to the practice-ground. There were more than Mrs. Corporal Morrison who felt as she did. But Cottar was busy for eleven hours of the day. He did not care to have his tennis spoiled by petticoats in the court; and after one long afternoon at a garden-party, he explained to his major that this sort of thing was "futile piffle," and the major laughed. Theirs was not a married mess, except for the colonel's wife, and Cottar stood in awe of the good lady. She said "my regiment," and the world knows what that means. None the less, when they wanted her to give away the prizes after a shooting-match, and she refused because one of the prize-winners was married to a girl who had made a jest of her behind her broad back, the mess ordered Cottar to "tackle her," in his best calling-kit. This he did, simply and laboriously, and she gave way altogether.

"She only wanted to know the facts of the case," he explained. "I just told her, and she saw at once."

"Ye-es," said the adjutant. "I expect that's what she did. Comin' to the Fusiliers' dance to-night, Galahad?"

"No, thanks. I've got a fight on with the major." The virtuous apprentice sat up till midnight in the major's quarters, with a stop-watch and a pair of compasses, shifting little painted lead-blocks about a four-inch map.

Then he turned in and slept the sleep of innocence, which is full of healthy dreams. One peculiarity of his dreams he noticed at the beginning of his second hot weather. Two or three

times a month they duplicated or ran in series.
He would find himself sliding into dreamland by
the same road — a road that ran along a beach
near a pile of brushwood. To the right lay the
sea, sometimes at full tide, sometimes withdrawn
to the very horizon; but he knew it for the same
sea. By that road he would travel over a swell of
rising ground covered with short, withered grass,
into valleys of wonder and unreason. Beyond the
ridge, which was crowned with some sort of street-
lamp, anything was possible; but up to the lamp
it seemed to him that he knew the road as well as
he knew the parade-ground. He learned to look
forward to the place; for, once there, he was sure
of a good night's rest, and Indian hot weather can
be rather trying. First, shadowy under closing
eyelids, would come the outline of the brushwood-
pile; next the white sand of the beach-road, almost
overhanging the black, changeful sea; then the
turn inland and uphill to the single light. When
he was unrestful for any reason, he would tell
himself how he was sure to get there — sure to
get there — if he shut his eyes and surrendered
to the drift of things. But one night after a foolishly hard hour's polo (the thermometer was 94°
in his quarters at ten o'clock), sleep stood away
from him altogether, though he did his best to find
the well-known road, the point where true sleep
began. At last he saw the brushwood-pile, and

hurried along to the ridge, for behind him he felt was the wide-awake, sultry world. He reached the lamp in safety, tingling with drowsiness, when a policeman — a common country policeman — sprang up before him and touched him on the shoulder ere he could dive into the dim valley below. He was filled with terror,— the hopeless terror of dreams,— for the policeman said, in the awful, distinct voice of dream-people, "I am Policeman Day coming back from the City of Sleep. You come with me." Georgie knew it was true — that just beyond him in the valley lay the lights of the City of Sleep, where he would have been sheltered, and that this Policeman-Thing had full power and authority to head him back to miserable wakefulness. He found himself looking at the moonlight on the wall, dripping with fright; and he never overcame that horror, though he met the Policeman several times that hot weather, and his coming was the forerunner of a bad night.

But other dreams — perfectly absurd ones — filled him with an incommunicable delight. All those that he remembered began by the brush-wood-pile. For instance, he found a small clock-work steamer (he had noticed it many nights before) lying by the sea-road, and stepped into it, whereupon it moved with surpassing swiftness over an absolutely level sea. This was glorious, for he felt he was exploring great matters; and it stopped by a lily carved in stone, which, most naturally, floated on the water. Seeing the lily was labelled "Hong-Kong," Georgie said: "Of course. This is precisely what I expected Hong-Kong would be like. How magnificent!" Thousands of miles farther on it halted at yet another stone lily, labelled "Java"; and this, again, delighted him hugely, because he knew that now he was at the world's end. But the little boat ran on and on till it lay in a deep fresh-water lock, the sides of which were carven marble, green with moss. Lily-pads lay on the water, and reeds arched above. Some one moved among the reeds — some one whom Georgie knew he had travelled to this world's end to reach. Therefore everything was entirely well with him. He was unspeakably happy, and vaulted over the ship's side to find this person. When his feet touched that still water, it changed, with the rustle of unrolling maps, to nothing less than a sixth quarter of the globe, beyond the most remote imagining of man — a place where islands were coloured yellow and blue, their lettering strung across their faces. They gave on unknown seas, and Georgie's urgent desire was to return swiftly across this floating atlas to known bearings. He told himself repeatedly that it was no good to hurry; but still he hurried desperately, and the islands slipped and slid under his feet, the straits yawned and widened, till he found himself utterly lost in the world's fourth dimension, with no hope of return. Yet only a little distance away he could see the old world with the rivers and mountain-chains marked according to the Sandhurst rules of map-making. Then that person for whom he had come to the Lily Lock (that was its name) ran up across unexplored territories, and showed him a way. They fled hand in hand till they reached a road that spanned ravines, and ran along the edge of precipices, and was tunnelled through mountains. "This goes to our brushwood-pile," said his companion; and all his trouble was at an end. He took a pony, because he understood that this was the Thirty-Mile Ride and he must ride swiftly, and raced through the clattering tunnels and round the curves, always downhill, till he heard the sea to his left, and saw it raging under a full moon, against sandy cliffs. It was heavy going, but he recognised the nature of the country, the dark-purple downs inland, and the bents that whistled in the wind. The road was eaten away in places, and the sea lashed at him— black, foamless tongues of smooth and glossy rollers; but he was sure that there was less danger from the sea than from "Them," whoever "They" were, inland to his right. He knew, too, that he would be safe if he could reach the down with the lamp on it. This came as he expected: he saw the one light a mile ahead along the beach, dismounted, turned to the right, walked quietly over to the brushwood-pile, found the little steamer had returned to the beach whence he had unmoored it, and — must have fallen asleep, for he could remember no more. "I'm gettin' the hang of the geography of that place," he said to himself, as he shaved next morning. "I must have made some sort of circle. Let's see. The Thirty-Mile Ride (now how the deuce did I know it was called the Thirty-Mile Ride?) joins the sea-road beyond the first down where the lamp is. And that atlas-country lies at the back of the Thirty-Mile Ride, somewhere out to the right beyond the hills and tunnels. Rummy things, dreams. 'Wonder what makes mine fit into each other so?"

He continued on his solid way through the recurring duties of the seasons. The regiment was shifted to another station, and he enjoyed road-marching for two months, with a good deal of mixed shooting thrown in, and when they reached their new cantonments he became a member of the local Tent Club, and chased the mighty boar on horseback with a short stabbing-spear. There he met the *mahseer* of the Poonch, beside whom the tarpon is as a herring, and he who lands him can say that he is a fisherman. This was as new and as fascinating as the big-game shooting that fell to his portion, when he had himself photographed for the mother's benefit, sitting on the flank of his first tiger.

Then the adjutant was promoted, and Cottar rejoiced with him, for he admired the adjutant greatly, and marvelled who might be big enough to fill his place; so that he nearly collapsed when the mantle fell on his own shoulders, and the colonel said a few sweet things that made him blush. An adjutant's position does not differ materially from that of head of the school, and Cottar stood in the same relation to the colonel as he had to his old Head in England. Only, tempers wear out in hot weather, and things were said and done that tried him sorely, and he made glorious blunders, from which the regimental sergeant-major pulled him with a loyal soul and a shut mouth. Slovens and incompetents raged against him; the weak-minded strove to lure him from the ways of justice; the small-minded — yea, men whom Cottar believed would never do "things no fellow can do "— imputed motives mean and circuitous to actions that he had not spent a thought upon; and he tasted injustice, and it made him very sick. But his consolation came on parade, when he looked down the full companies, and reflected how few were in hospital or cells, and wondered when the time would come to try the machine of his love and labour.

But they needed and expected the whole of a man's working-day, and maybe three or four hours of the night. Curiously enough, he never dreamed about the regiment as he was popularly supposed to. The mind, set free from the day's doings, generally ceased working altogether, or, if it moved at all, carried him along the old beach-road to the downs, the lamp-post, and, once in a while, to terrible Policeman Day. The second time that he returned to the world's lost continent (this was a dream that repeated itself again and again, with variations, on the same ground) he knew that if he only sat still the person from the Lily Lock would help him, and he was not disappointed. Sometimes he was trapped in mines of vast depth hollowed out of the heart of the world, where men in torment chanted echoing songs; and he heard this person coming along through the galleries, and everything was made safe and delightful. They met again in low-roofed Indian railway-carriages that halted in a garden surrounded by gilt-and-green railings, where a mob of stony white people, all unfriendly, sat at breakfast-tables covered with roses, and separated Georgie from his companion, while underground voices sang deep-voiced songs. Georgie was filled with enormous despair till they two met again. They foregathered in the middle of an endless, hot tropic night, and crept into a huge house that stood, he knew, somewhere north of the railway-station where the people ate among the roses. It was surrounded with gardens, all moist and dripping; and in one room, reached through leagues of whitewashed passages, a Sick Thing lay in bed. Now the least noise, Georgie knew, would unchain some waiting horror, and his companion knew it, too; but when their eyes met across the bed, Georgie was disgusted to see that she was a child—a little girl in strapped shoes, with her black hair combed back from her forehead.

"What disgraceful folly!" he thought. "Now she could do nothing whatever if Its head came off."

Then the Thing coughed, and the ceiling shattered down in plaster on the mosquito-netting, and "They" rushed in from all quarters. He dragged the child through the stifling garden, voices chanting behind them, and they rode the Thirty-Mile Ride under whip and spur along the sandy beach by the booming sea, till they came to the downs, the lamp-post, and the brushwood-pile, which was safety. Very often dreams would break up about them in this fashion, and they would be separated, to endure awful adventures alone. But the most amusing times were when he and she had a clear understanding that it was all make-believe, and walked through mile-wide roaring rivers without even taking off their shoes, or set light to populous cities to see how they would burn, and were rude as any children to the vague shadows met in their rambles. Later in the night they were sure to suffer for this, either at the hands of the Railway People eating among the roses, or in the tropic uplands at the far end of the Thirty-Mile Ride. Together, this did not much affright them; but often Georgie would hear her shrill cry of "Boy! Boy!" half a world away, and hurry to her rescue before "They" maltreated her.

He and she explored the dark-purple downs as far inland from the brushwood-pile as they dared, but that was always a dangerous matter. The interior was filled with "Them," and "They" went about singing in the hollows, and Georgie and she felt safer on or near the seaboard. So thoroughly had he come to know the place of his dreams that even waking he accepted it as a real country, and made a rough sketch of it. He kept his own counsel, of course; but the permanence of the land puzzled him. His ordinary dreams were as formless and as fleeting as any healthy dreams could be, but once at the brushwood-pile he moved within known limits and could see where he was going. There were months at a time when nothing notable crossed his sleep. Then the dreams would come in a batch of five or six, and next morning the map that he kept in his writing-case would be written up to date, for Georgie was a most methodical person. There was, indeed, a danger — his seniors said so — of his developing into a regular "Auntie Fuss" of an adjutant, and

when an officer once takes to old-maidism there is more hope for the virgin of seventy than for him.

But fate sent the change that was needed, in the shape of a little winter campaign on the Border, which, after the manner of little campaigns, flashed out into a very ugly war; and Cottar's regiment was chosen among the first.

"Now," said a major, "this'll shake the cobwebs out of us all — especially you, Galahad; and we can see what your hen-with-one-chick attitude has done for the regiment."

Cottar nearly wept with joy as the campaign went forward. They were fit — physically fit beyond the other troops; they were good children in camp, wet or dry, fed or unfed; and they followed their officers with the quick suppleness and trained obedience of a first-class football fifteen. They were cut off from their apology for a base, and cheerfully cut their way back to it again; they crowned and cleaned out hills full of the enemy with the precision of well-broken dogs of chase; and in the hour of retreat, when, hampered with the sick and wounded of the column, they were persecuted down eleven miles of waterless valley, they, serving as rear-guard, covered themselves with a great glory in the eyes of fellow-professionals. Any regiment can advance, but few know how to retreat with a sting in the tail. Then they turned to make roads, most often under fire, and dismantled some inconvenient mud redoubts. They were the last corps to be withdrawn when the rubbish of the campaign was all swept up; and after a month in standing camp, which tries

morals severely, they departed to their own place
in column of fours, singing:

    " 'E's goin' to do without 'em —
      Don't want 'em any more;
    'E's goin' to do without 'em,
      As 'e's often done before.
    'E's goin' to be a martyr
    On a 'ighly novel plan,
    An' all the boys and girls will say,
    ' Ow! what a nice young man — man — man!
      Ow! what a nice young man!' "

There came out a "Gazette" in which Cottar
found that he had been behaving with "courage
and coolness and discretion" in all his capacities;
that he had assisted the wounded under fire, and
blown in a gate, also under fire. Net result, his
captaincy and a brevet majority, coupled with the
Distinguished Service Order.

As to his wounded, he explained that they were
both heavy men, whom he could lift more easily
than any one else. "Otherwise, of course, I should
have sent out one of my men; and, of course,
about that gate business, we were safe the minute
we were well under the walls." But this did not
prevent his men from cheering him furiously
whenever they saw him, or the mess from giving
him a dinner on the eve of his departure to
England. (A year's leave was among the things
he had "snaffled out of the campaign," to use

his own words.) The doctor, who had taken quite as much as was good for him, quoted poetry about " a good blade carving the casques of men," and so on, and everybody told Cottar that he was an excellent person; but when he rose to make his maiden speech they shouted so that he was understood to say, " It isn't any use tryin' to speak with you chaps rottin' me like this. Let's have some pool."

* * * * * * * * * *

It is not unpleasant to spend eight-and-twenty days in an easy-going steamer on warm waters, in the company of a woman who lets you see that you are head and shoulders superior to the rest of the world, even though that woman may be, and most often is, ten counted years your senior. P.& O. boats are not lighted with the disgustful particularity of Atlantic liners. There is more phosphorescence at the bows, and greater silence and darkness by the hand-steering gear aft.

Awful things might have happened to Georgie but for the little fact that he had never studied the first principles of the game he was expected to play. So when Mrs. Zuleika, at Aden, told him how motherly an interest she felt in his welfare, medals, brevet, and all, Georgie took her at the foot of the letter, and promptly talked of his own mother, three hundred miles nearer each day, of his home, and so forth, all the way up the Red

Sea. It was much easier than he had supposed to converse with a woman for an hour at a time. Then Mrs. Zuleika, turning from parental affection, spoke of love in the abstract as a thing not unworthy of study, and in discreet twilights after dinner demanded confidences. Georgie would have been delighted to supply them, but he had none, and did not know it was his duty to manufacture them. Mrs. Zuleika expressed surprise and unbelief, and asked those questions which deep asks of deep. She learned all that was necessary to conviction, and, being very much a woman, resumed (Georgie never knew that she had abandoned) the motherly attitude.

"Do you know," she said, somewhere in the Mediterranean, "I think you're the very dearest boy I have ever met in my life, and I'd like you to remember me a little. You will when you are older, but I want you to remember me now. You'll make some girl very happy."

"Oh! 'Hope so," said Georgie, gravely; "but there's heaps of time for marryin' an' all that sort of thing, ain't there?"

"That depends. Here are your bean-bags for the Ladies' Competition. I think I'm growing too old to care for these *tamashas*."

They were getting up sports, and Georgie was on the committee. He never noticed how perfectly the bags were sewn, but another woman did, and smiled — once. He liked Mrs. Zuleika greatly. She was a bit old, of course, but uncommonly nice. There was no nonsense about her.

A few nights after they passed Gibraltar his dream returned to him. She who waited by the brushwood-pile was no longer a little girl, but a woman with black hair that grew into a " widow's peak," combed back from her forehead. He knew her for the child in black, the companion of the last six years, and, as it had been in the time of the meetings on the Lost Continent, he was filled with delight unspeakable. " They," for some dreamland reason, were friendly or had gone away that night, and the two flitted together over all their country, from the brushwood-pile up the Thirty-Mile Ride, till they saw the House of the Sick Thing, a pin-point in the distance to the left; stamped through the Railway Waiting-room where the roses lay on the spread breakfast-tables; and returned, by the ford and the city they had once burned for sport, to the great swells of the downs under the lamp-post. Wherever they moved a strong singing followed them underground, but this night there was no panic. All the land was empty except for themselves, and at the last (they were sitting by the lamp-post hand in hand) she turned and kissed him. He woke with a start, staring at the waving curtain of the cabin door; he could almost have sworn that the kiss was real.

Next morning the ship was rolling in a Biscay sea, and people were not happy; but as Georgie came to breakfast, shaven, tubbed, and smelling of soap, several turned to look at him because of the light in his eyes and the splendour of his countenance.

"Well, you look beastly fit," snapped a neighbour. "Any one left you a legacy in the middle of the Bay?"

Georgie reached for the curry, with a seraphic grin. "I suppose it's the gettin' so near home, and all that. I do feel rather festive this mornin'. 'Rolls a bit, doesn't she?"

Mrs. Zuleika stayed in her cabin till the end of the voyage, when she left without bidding him farewell, and wept passionately on the dock-head for pure joy of meeting her children, who, she had often said, were so like their father.

Georgie headed for his own country, wild with delight of his first long furlough after the lean seasons. Nothing was changed in that orderly life, from the coachman who met him at the station to the white peacock that stormed at the carriage from the stone wall above the shaven lawns. The house took toll of him with due regard to precedence — first the mother; then the father; then the housekeeper, who wept and praised God;

then the butler, and so on down to the under-
keeper, who had been dog-boy in Georgie's youth,
and called him "Master Georgie," and was re-
proved by the groom who had taught Georgie to
ride.

"Not a thing changed," he sighed contentedly,
when the three of them sat down to dinner in the
late sunlight, while the rabbits crept out upon
the lawn below the cedars, and the big trout in
the ponds by the home paddock rose for their
evening meal.

"*Our* changes are all over, dear," cooed the
mother; "and now I am getting used to your size
and your tan (you're very brown, Georgie), I see
you haven't changed in the least. You're exactly
like the pater."

The father beamed on this man after his own
heart,—"youngest major in the army, and should
have had the V. C., sir,"—and the butler listened
with his professional mask off when Master
Georgie spoke of war as it is waged to-day, and
his father cross-questioned.

They went out on the terrace to smoke among
the roses, and the shadow of the old house lay
long across the wonderful English foliage, which
is the only living green in the world.

"Perfect! By Jove, it's perfect!" Georgie was
looking at the round-bosomed woods beyond the
home paddock, where the white pheasant boxes

281

were ranged; and the golden air was full of a hundred sacred scents and sounds. Georgie felt his father's arm tighten in his.

"It's not half bad — but *hodie mihi, cras tibi*, isn't it? I suppose you'll be turning up some fine day with a girl under your arm, if you haven't one now, eh?"

"You can make your mind easy, sir. I haven't one."

"Not in all these years?" said the mother.

"I hadn't time, mummy. They keep a man pretty busy, these days, in the service, and most of our mess are unmarried, too."

"But you must have met hundreds in society — at balls, and so on?"

"I'm like the Tenth, mummy: I don't dance."

"Don't dance! What have you been doing with yourself, then — backing other men's bills?" said the father.

"Oh, yes; I've done a little of that too; but you see, as things are now, a man has all his work cut out for him to keep abreast of his profession, and my days were always too full to let me lark about half the night."

"Hmm!"— suspiciously.

"It's never too late to learn. We ought to give some kind of housewarming for the people about, now you've come back. Unless you want to go straight up to town, dear?"

"No. I don't want anything better than this. Let's sit still and enjoy ourselves. I suppose there will be something for me to ride if I look for it?"

"Seeing I've been kept down to the old brown pair for the last six weeks because all the others were being got ready for Master Georgie, I should say there might be," the father chuckled. "They're reminding me in a hundred ways that I must take the second place now."

"Brutes!"

"The pater doesn't mean it, dear; but every one has been trying to make your home-coming a success; and you *do* like it, don't you?"

"Perfect! Perfect! There's no place like England — when you've done your work."

"That's the proper way to look at it, my son."

And so up and down the flagged walk till their shadows grew long in the moonlight, and the mother went indoors and played such songs as a small boy once clamoured for, and the squat silver candlesticks were brought in, and Georgie climbed to the two rooms in the west wing that had been his nursery and his playroom in the beginning. Then who should come to tuck him up for the night but the mother? And she sat down on the bed, and they talked for a long hour, as mother and son should, if there is to be any future for the Empire. With a simple woman's deep guile she asked questions and suggested answers that should have waked some sign in the face on the pillow, and there was neither quiver of eyelid nor quickening of breath, neither evasion nor delay in reply. So she blessed him and kissed him on the mouth, which is not always a mother's property, and said something to her husband later, at which he laughed profane and incredulous laughs.

All the establishment waited on Georgie next morning, from the tallest six-year-old, "with a mouth like a kid glove, Master Georgie," to the under-keeper strolling carelessly along the horizon, Georgie's pet rod in his hand, and "There's a four-pounder risin' below the lasher. You don't 'ave 'em in Injia, Mast — Major Georgie." It was all beautiful beyond telling, even though the mother insisted on taking him out in the landau (the leather had the hot Sunday smell of his youth) and showing him off to her friends at all the houses for six miles round; and the pater bore him up to town and a lunch at the club, where he introduced him, quite carelessly, to not less than thirty ancient warriors whose sons were not the youngest majors in the army and had not the D. S. O. After that it was Georgie's turn; and remembering his friends, he filled up the house with that kind of officer who live in cheap lodgings at Southsea or Montpelier Square, Brompton — good men all, but not well off. The mother perceived that they

needed girls to play with; and as there was no
scarcity of girls, the house hummed like a dove-
cote in spring. They tore up the place for ama-
teur theatricals; they disappeared in the gardens
when they ought to have been rehearsing; they
swept off every available horse and vehicle, especially the governess-cart and the fat pony; they
fell into the trout-ponds; they picnicked and they
tennised; and they sat on gates in the twilight,
two by two, and Georgie found that he was not in
the least necessary to their entertainment.

"My word!" said he, when he saw the last of
their dear backs. "They told me they've enjoyed
'emselves, but they haven't done half the things
they said they would."

"I know they've enjoyed themselves — immensely," said the mother. "You're a public
benefactor, dear."

"Now we can be quiet again, can't we?"

"Oh, quite. I've a very dear friend of mine
that I want you to know. She couldn't come
with the house so full, because she's an invalid,
and she was away when you first came. She's a
Mrs. Lacy."

"Lacy! I don't remember the name about
here."

"No; they came after you went to India —
from Oxford. Her husband died there, and she
lost some money, I believe. They bought The

285

Firs on the Bassett Road. She's a very sweet woman, and we're very fond of them both."

"She's a widow, didn't you say?"

"She has a daughter. Surely I said so, dear?"

"Does she fall into trout-ponds, and gas and giggle, and 'Oh, Major Cottah!' and all that sort of thing?"

"No, indeed. She's a very quiet girl, and very musical. She always came over here with her music-books — composing, you know; and she generally works all day, so you won't —"

"'Talking about Miriam?" said the pater, coming up. The mother edged towards him within elbow-reach. There was no finesse about Georgie's father. "Oh, Miriam's a dear girl. Plays beautifully. Rides beautifully, too. She's a regular pet of the household. Used to call me —" The elbow went home, and ignorant but obedient always, the pater shut himself off.

"What used she to call you, sir?"

"All sorts of pet names. I'm very fond of Miriam."

"'Sounds Jewish — Miriam."

"Jew! You'll be calling yourself a Jew next. She's one of the Herefordshire Lacys. When her aunt dies —" Again the elbow.

"Oh, you won't see anything of her, Georgie. She's busy with her music or her mother all day. Besides, you're going up to town to-morrow, aren't you? I thought you said something about an Institute meeting?" The mother spoke.

"Go up to town *now!* What nonsense!" Once more the pater was shut off.

"I had some idea of it, but I'm not quite sure," said the son of the house. Why did the mother try to get him away because a musical girl and her invalid parent were expected? He did not approve of unknown females calling his father pet names. He would observe these pushing persons who had been only seven years in the county.

All of which the delighted mother read in his countenance, herself keeping an air of sweet disinterestedness.

"They'll be here this evening for dinner. I'm sending the carriage over for them, and they won't stay more than a week."

"Perhaps I shall go up to town. I don't quite know yet." Georgie moved away irresolutely. There was a lecture at the United Services Institute on the supply of ammunition in the field, and the one man whose theories most irritated Major Cottar would deliver it. A heated discussion was sure to follow, and perhaps he might find himself moved to speak. He took his rod that afternoon and went down to thrash it out among the trout.

"Good sport, dear!" said the mother, from the terrace.

" 'Fraid it won't be, mummy. All those men from town, and the girls particularly, have put every trout off his feed for weeks. There isn't one of 'em that cares for fishin'— really. Fancy stampin' and shoutin' on the bank, and tellin' every fish for half a mile exactly what you're goin' to do, and then chuckin' a brute of a fly at him! By Jove, it would scare *me* if I was a trout!"

But things were not as bad as he had expected. The black gnat was on the water, and the water was strictly preserved. A three-quarter-pounder at the second cast set him for the campaign, and he worked down-stream, crouching behind the reed and meadow-sweet; creeping between a horn-beam hedge and a foot-wide strip of bank, where he could see the trout, but where they could not distinguish him from the background; lying almost on his stomach to switch the blue-upright sidewise through the checkered shadows of a gravelly ripple under overarching trees. But he had known every inch of the water since he was four feet high. The aged and astute between sunk roots, with the large and fat that lay in the frothy scum below some strong rush of water, sucking as lazily as carp, came to trouble in their turn, at the hand that imitated so delicately the flicker and wimple of an egg-dropping fly. Consequently, Georgie found himself five miles from home when he ought to have been dressing for dinner. The housekeeper had taken good care that her boy should not go empty, and before he changed to the white moth he sat down to excellent claret with sandwiches of potted egg and things that adoring women make and men never notice. Then back, to surprise the otter grubbing for fresh-water mussels, the rabbits on the edge of the beechwoods foraging in the clover, and the policeman-like white owl stooping to the little field-mice, till the moon was strong, and he took his rod apart, and went home through well-remembered gaps in the hedges. He fetched a compass round the house, for, though he might have broken every law of the establishment every hour, the law of his boyhood was unbreakable: after fishing you went in by the south garden back-door, cleaned up in the outer scullery, and did not present yourself to your elders and your betters till you had washed and changed.

"Half-past ten, by Jove! Well, we'll make the sport an excuse. They wouldn't want to see me the first evening, at any rate. Gone to bed, probably." He skirted by the open French windows of the drawing-room. "No, they haven't. They look very comfy in there."

He could see his father in his own particular chair, the mother in hers, and the back of a girl at the piano by the big potpourri-jar. The gar-

THE BRUSHWOOD BOY

dens looked half divine in the moonlight, and he
turned down through the roses to finish his pipe.

A prelude ended, and there floated out a voice
of the kind that in his childhood he used to call
"creamy"—a full, true contralto; and this is the
song that he heard, every syllable of it:

> Over the edge of the purple down,
>   Where the single lamplight gleams,
> Know ye the road to the Merciful Town
>   That is hard by the Sea of Dreams—
> Where the poor may lay their wrongs away,
>   And the sick may forget to weep?
> But we—pity us! Oh, pity us!
>   We wakeful; ah, pity us!—
> We must go back with Policeman Day—
>   Back from the City of Sleep!
>
> Weary they turn from the scroll and crown,
>   Fetter and prayer and plough—
> They that go up to the Merciful Town,
>   For her gates are closing now.
> It is their right in the Baths of Night
>   Body and soul to steep:
> But we—pity us! ah, pity us!
>   We wakeful; oh, pity us!—
> We must go back with Policeman Day—
>   Back from the City of Sleep!
>
> Over the edge of the purple down,
>   Ere the tender dreams begin,
> Look—we may look—at the Merciful Town,
>   But we may not enter in!

290

> Outcasts all, from her guarded wall
>   Back to our watch we creep:
> We — pity us! ah, pity us!
>   We wakeful; oh, pity us! —
> We that go back with Policeman Day —
>   Back from the City of Sleep!

At the last echo he was aware that his mouth was dry and unknown pulses were beating in the roof of it. The housekeeper, who would have it that he must have fallen in and caught a chill, was waiting to catch him on the stairs, and, since he neither saw nor answered her, carried a wild tale abroad that brought his mother knocking at the door.

"Anything happened, dear? Harper said she thought you weren't — "

"No; it's nothing. I'm all right, mummy. *Please* don't bother."

He did not recognise his own voice, but that was a small matter beside what he was considering. Obviously, most obviously, the whole coincidence was crazy lunacy. He proved it to the satisfaction of Major George Cottar, who was going up to town to-morrow to hear a lecture on the supply of ammunition in the field; and having so proved it, the soul and brain and heart and body of Georgie cried joyously: " That's the Lily Lock girl — the Lost Continent girl — the Thirty-Mile Ride girl! —the Brushwood girl! *I* know her! "

He waked, stiff and cramped in his chair, to reconsider the situation by sunlight, when it did not appear normal. But a man must eat, and he went to breakfast, his heart between his teeth, holding himself severely in hand.

"Late, as usual," said the mother. "'My boy, Miss Lacy."

A tall girl in black raised her eyes to his, and Georgie's life training deserted him —just as soon as he realised that she did not know. He stared coolly and critically. There was the abundant black hair, growing in a widow's peak, turned back from the forehead, with that peculiar ripple over the right ear; there were the grey eyes set a little close together; the short upper lip, resolute chin, and the known poise of the head. There was also the small well-cut mouth that had kissed him.

"Georgie — *dear!*" said the mother, amazedly, for Miriam was flushing under the stare.

"I — I beg your pardon!" he gulped. "I don't know whether the mother has told you, but I'm rather an idiot at times, specially before I've had my breakfast. It's — it's a family failing."

He turned to explore among the hot-water dishes on the sideboard, rejoicing that she did not know — she did not know.

His conversation for the rest of the meal was mildly insane, though the mother thought she had never seen her boy look half so handsome. How could any girl, least of all one of Miriam's discernment, forbear to fall down and worship? But deeply Miriam was displeased. She had never been stared at in that fashion before, and promptly retired into her shell when Georgie announced that he had changed his mind about going to town, and would stay to play with Miss Lacy if she had nothing better to do.

" Oh, but don't let me throw you out. I'm at work. I've things to do all the morning."

" What possessed Georgie to behave so oddly?" the mother sighed to herself. " Miriam's a bundle of feelings — like her mother."

" You compose — don't you? Must be a fine thing to be able to do that. [" Pig — oh, pig!" thought Miriam.] I think I heard you singin' when I came in last night after fishin'. All about a Sea of Dreams, wasn't it? [Miriam shuddered to the core of the soul that afflicted her.] Awfully pretty song. How d' you think of such things?"

" You only composed the music, dear, didn't you?"

" The words too. I'm sure of it," said Georgie, with a sparkling eye. No; she did not know.

" Yeth; I wrote the words too." Miriam spoke slowly, for she knew she lisped when she was nervous.

" Now how *could* you tell, Georgie?" said the mother, as delighted as though the youngest major in the army were ten years old, showing off before company.

"I was sure of it, somehow. Oh, there are heaps of things about me, mummy, that you don't understand. 'Looks as if it were goin' to be a hot day — for England. Would you care for a ride this afternoon, Miss Lacy? We can start out after tea, if you'd like it."

Miriam could not in decency refuse, but any woman might see she was not filled with delight.

"That will be very nice, if you take the Bassett Road. It will save me sending Martin down to the village," said the mother, filling in gaps.

Like all good managers, the mother had her one weakness — a mania for little strategies that should economise horses and vehicles. Her men-folk complained that she turned them into common carriers, and there was a legend in the family that she had once said to the pater on the morning of a meet: "If you *should* kill near Bassett, dear, and if it isn't too late, would you mind just popping over and matching me this?"

"I knew that was coming. You'd never miss a chance, mother. If it's a fish or a trunk I won't." Georgie laughed.

"It's only a duck. They can do it up very neatly at Mallett's," said the mother, simply. "You won't mind, will you? We'll have a scratch dinner at nine, because it's so hot."

The long summer day dragged itself out for centuries; but at last there was tea on the lawn, and Miriam appeared.

She was in the saddle before he could offer to help, with the clean spring of the child who mounted the pony for the Thirty-Mile Ride. The day held mercilessly, though Georgie got down thrice to look for imaginary stones in Rufus's foot. One cannot say even simple things in broad light, and this that Georgie meditated was not simple. So he spoke seldom, and Miriam was divided between relief and scorn. It annoyed her that the great hulking thing should know she had written the words of the song overnight; for though a maiden may sing her most secret fancies aloud, she does not care to have them trampled over by the male Philistine. They rode into the little red-brick street of Bassett, and Georgie made untold fuss over the disposition of that duck. It must go in just such a package, and be fastened to the saddle in just such a manner, though eight o'clock had struck and they were miles from dinner.

"We must be quick!" said Miriam, bored and angry.

"There's no great hurry; but we can cut over Dowhead Down, and let 'em out on the grass. That will save us half an hour."

The horses capered on the short, sweet-smelling

turf, and the delaying shadows gathered in the valley as they cantered over the great dun down that overhangs Bassett and the Western coaching-road. Insensibly the pace quickened without thought of mole-hills; Rufus, gentleman that he was, waiting on Miriam's Dandy till they should have cleared the rise. Then down the two-mile slope they raced together, the wind whistling in their ears, to the steady throb of eight hooves and the light click-click of the shifting bits.

"Oh, that was glorious!" Miriam cried, reining in. "Dandy and I are old friends, but I don't think we've ever gone better together."

"No; but you've gone quicker, once or twice."

"Really? When?"

Georgie moistened his lips. "Don't you remember the Thirty-Mile Ride — with me — when 'They' were after us — on the beach-road, with the sea to the left — going towards the lamp-post on the downs?"

The girl gasped. "What — what do you mean?" she said hysterically.

"The Thirty-Mile Ride, and — and all the rest of it."

"You mean —? I didn't sing anything about the Thirty-Mile Ride. I know I didn't. I have never told a living soul."

"You told about Policeman Day, and the lamp at the top of the downs, and the City of Sleep.

It all joins on, you know — it's the same country — and it was easy enough to see where you had been."

"Good God! — It joins on — of course it does; but — I have been — you have been — Oh, let's walk, please, or I shall fall off!"

Georgie ranged alongside, and laid a hand that shook below her bridle-hand, pulling Dandy into a walk. Miriam was sobbing as he had seen a man sob under the touch of the bullet.

"It's all right — it's all right," he whispered feebly. "Only — only it's true, you know."

"True! Am I mad?"

"Not unless I'm mad as well. *Do* try to think a minute quietly. How could any one conceivably know anything about the Thirty-Mile Ride having anything to do with you, unless he had been there?"

"But where? But *where?* Tell me!"

"There — wherever it may be — in our country, I suppose. Do you remember the first time you rode it — the Thirty-Mile Ride, I mean? You must."

"It was all dreams — all dreams!"

"Yes, but tell, please; because I know."

"Let me think. I — we were on no account to make any noise — on no account to make any noise." She was staring between Dandy's ears, with eyes that did not see, and a suffocating heart.

"Because 'It' was dying in the big house?" Georgie went on, reining in again.

"There was a garden with green-and-gilt railings — all hot. Do *you* remember?"

"I ought to. I was sitting on the other side of the bed before 'It' coughed and 'They' came in."

"You!" — the deep voice was unnaturally full and strong, and the girl's wide-opened eyes burned in the dusk as she stared him through and through. "Then you're the Boy — my Brushwood Boy, and I've known you all my life!"

She fell forward on Dandy's neck. Georgie forced himself out of the weakness that was overmastering his limbs, and slid an arm round her waist. The head dropped on his shoulder, and he found himself with parched lips saying things that up till then he believed existed only in printed works of fiction. Mercifully the horses were quiet. She made no attempt to draw herself away when she recovered, but lay still, whispering, "Of course you're the Boy, and I didn't know — I didn't know."

"I knew last night; and when I saw you at breakfast — "

"Oh, *that* was why! I wondered at the time. You would, of course."

"I couldn't speak before this. Keep your head where it is, dear. It's all right now — all right now, isn't it?"

"But how was it *I* didn't know — after all these years and years? I remember — oh, what lots of things I remember!"

"Tell me some. I'll look after the horses."

"I remember waiting for you when the steamer came in. Do you?"

"At the Lily Lock, beyond Hong-Kong and Java?"

"Do *you* call it that, too?"

"You told me it was when I was lost in the continent. That was you that showed me the way through the mountains?"

"When the islands slid? It must have been, because you're the only one I remember. All the others were 'Them.'"

"Awful brutes they were, too."

"I remember showing you the Thirty-Mile Ride the first time. You ride just as you used to — then. You *are* you!"

"That's odd. I thought that of you this afternoon. Isn't it wonderful?"

"What does it all mean? Why should you and I of the millions of people in the world have this — this thing between us? What does it mean? I'm frightened."

"This!" said Georgie. The horses quickened their pace. They thought they had heard an order. "Perhaps when we die we may find out more, but it means this now."

There was no answer. What could she say? As the world went, they had known each other rather less than eight and a half hours, but the matter was one that did not concern the world. There was a very long silence, while the breath in their nostrils drew cold and sharp as it might have been a fume of ether.

" That's the second," Georgie whispered. " You remember, don't you?"

" It's not! " — furiously. " It's not!"

" On the downs the other night — months ago. You were just as you are now, and we went over the country for miles and miles."

" It was all empty, too. ' They' had gone away. Nobody frightened us. I wonder why, Boy?"

" Oh, if you remember *that*, you must remember the rest. Confess!"

" I remember lots of things, but I *know* I didn't. I never have — till just now."

" You *did*, dear."

" I know I didn't, because — oh, it's no use keeping anything back! — because I truthfully meant to."

" And truthfully did."

" No; meant to; but some one else came by."

" There wasn't any one else. There never has been."

" There was — there always is. It was another woman — out there on the sea. I saw her. It was the 26th of May. I've got it written down somewhere."

"Oh, *you've* kept a record of your dreams, too? That's odd about the other woman, because I happened to be on the sea just then."

"I was right. How do I know what you've done when you were awake — and I thought it was only *you!*"

"You never were more wrong in your life. What a little temper you've got! Listen to me a minute, dear." And Georgie, though he knew it not, committed black perjury. "It — it isn't the kind of thing one says to any one, because they'd laugh; but on my word and honour, darling, I've never been kissed by a living soul outside my own people in all my life. Don't laugh, dear. I wouldn't tell any one but you, but it's the solemn truth."

"I knew! You are you. Oh, I *knew* you'd come some day; but I didn't know you were you in the least till you spoke."

"Then give me another."

"And you never cared or looked anywhere? Why, all the round world must have loved you from the very minute they saw you, Boy."

"They kept it to themselves if they did. No; I never cared."

"And we shall be late for dinner — horribly

late. Oh, how can I look at you in the light before your mother — and mine!"

"We'll play you're Miss Lacy till the proper time comes. What's the shortest limit for people to get engaged? S'pose we have got to go through all the fuss of an engagement, haven't we?"

"Oh, I don't want to talk about that. It's so commonplace. I've thought of something that you don't know. I'm sure of it. What's my name?"

"Miri — no, it isn't, by Jove! Wait half a second, and it'll come back to me. You aren't — you can't? Why, *those* old tales — before I went to school! I've never thought of 'em from that day to this. Are you the original, only Annie*an*-louise?"

"It was what you always called me ever since the beginning. Oh! We've turned into the avenue, and we must be an hour late."

"What does it matter? The chain goes as far back as those days? It must, of course — of course it must. I've got to ride round with this pestilent old bird — confound him!"

" '"Ha! ha!" said the duck, laughing' — do you remember *that?*"

"Yes, I do — flower-pots on my feet, and all. We've been together all this while; and I've got to say good-bye to you till dinner. *Sure* I'll see you at dinner-time? *Sure* you won't sneak up to your room, darling, and leave me all the evening? Good-bye, dear — good-bye."

"Good-bye, Boy, good-bye. Mind the arch! Don't let Rufus bolt into his stables. Good-bye. Yes, I'll come down to dinner; but — what shall I do when I see you in the light!"